Prey of the Corrupted Alpha

Ashlynn Carter

Copyright © 2024 by Ashlynn Carter

All rights reserved.

No part of this publication may be reproduced, distributed, or transmitted in any form or by any means, including photocopying, recording, or other electronic or mechanical methods, without the prior written permission of the publisher, except as permitted by U.S. copyright law. For permission requests, contact Ashlynn Carter at ashlynn.carter@proton.me.

The story, all names, characters, and incidents portrayed in this production are fictitious. No identification with actual persons (living or deceased), places, buildings, and products is intended or should be inferred.

Book Cover by Ashlynn Carter

First edition 2024

*For my daughters, who are as
Feisty and full of life as Carly and Cora*

Chapter 1

The day was warm with a light breeze and the clouds above me floated lazily across the clear blue sky. Perfect days like this were not going to last much longer. Bird songs mixed with the sound of the waterfall, adding to the calming atmosphere of the forest. This close to the border of the neighboring pack was usually quiet with very few visitors. That is why I loved this spot so much.

I sighed as I reclined back against my backpack. I was laying on my towel next to the small pool that the waterfall poured into, soaking up the sunshine while reading my book for school. Something about this place always brought me peace and helped to clear my mind.

I turned a page in the book as the alarm on my phone went off. Time to go. I put my bookmark in place before turning and tucking the book into my backpack. I pulled out the tank top I used for working out before stripping my shirt off to change.

A stick broke behind me and I froze for a second before I frantically pulled my tank top on. I decided against pulling out my sweatpants that I usually had on over my spandex shorts. It would take too long, and something told me I needed to be ready to run. I zipped my backpack closed as I stood quickly, scanning the forest behind me where the sound had come from.

"We are not alone." Cora, my wolf, said in my mind.

Usually, a werewolf didn't get their wolf until their eighteenth birthday. Cora and I were a little different. We have been able to communicate with each other since my sixteenth birthday, but we still did not have any of our wolf senses. I didn't have heightened strength or speed or hearing. I hadn't told anyone about Cora yet. I was already an outcast; I didn't need to give my tormentors any more reason to single me out.

"Was it the stick breaking that clued you in?" I asked sarcastically.

"Well, well, well. Looks like we found our mystery wolf." A man stepped out of the trees that bordered the neighboring pack. I had never seen him, or the other two men that followed him, before. I took a step to the side to try to prevent them from caging me in against the waterfall's pool that was behind me. "You are quite the beauty." His eyes traveled up and down my body.

The first man was tall with blonde hair. He didn't seem much older than I was. His shirt was pulled tight over his broad shoulders. He looked like a freaking bodybuilder. He also had a strong aura marking him as a higher-ranking wolf. His blue eyes darkened as they took me in.

The guy on his left laughed as he looked me up and down. He wore his muddy brown hair long enough to pull into a ponytail that reached his waist, and he had a scar that ran down his right cheek. He looked at me as if I were a feast he could not wait to devour. Granted, I was wearing a loose-fitting exercise tank-top and tight spandex shorts that barely reached mid-thigh, but still, I wasn't theirs to look at.

"She's definitely been worth the wait." the second man said as he licked his lips.

"Should we run?" I asked Cora as I eyed the three men slowly approaching. My heart rate increased with every step they took.

"Fight. We should definitely fight." Cora snarled. She was always looking for a good fight. Me, on the other hand, I preferred to avoid fighting at all costs.

"I thought you said no one came here?" A male voice said from behind me.

I froze. I knew that voice. I dreaded that voice. I glanced in its direction to see Easton Shepherd and Max Williams, two of my tormentors.

I was five when my mother and I moved into this pack, and Max, Mike, and Easton teased me nonstop. Easton was usually the instigator and actively sought me out throughout the day just to tease me.

I hadn't seen him since he left for training three months ago with the other higher-ranking wolves. That day he had teased me more than usual and then climbed in a car and left. I had been so upset that I went home and cried. It was strange. I missed Easton almost immediately, but I also felt relieved that he was not around to tease me. I still wasn't sure if the tears had come from his teasing, relief that he had gone, or the fact that he had gone and I wouldn't see him.

"I'm as surprised as you are." Max shrugged as they moved closer. While I was distracted by the new arrivals, the blonde man grabbed me by the waist and twisted me around, so I was facing him. He pulled me flush against him and I shoved at his chest to try to get away, but he held me too tight.

"Let go." I growled.

"Feisty, are we?" The man whispered as he nipped at my ear. "I like feisty." His hand began to slide lower and lower down my back until he grabbed my hip roughly.

"You do realize that he is three times our size, right?" Cora pointed out. *"There is no way you are going to just push him away."*

I raised my knee as hard as I could and connected right where I had hoped to. The man released me as he doubled over. I quickly backed several steps away, out of his reach.

I couldn't go far because Max and Easton had blocked my only exit. The man recovered quickly before glaring at me as he took a step in my direction. I took a matching step back but bumped into something hard.

I spun around to see what was behind me, only to find Easton. Easton glared down at me. He was bare chested, and I tried to move away from him, but before I could, he tugged his shirt down over my head. Blinking in surprise, I slipped my arms through the sleeves. An odd sense of comfort washed over me as Easton stepped around me, so that he and Max stood protectively between me and the three strangers. What was going on?

"What? Is she your mate or something?" The first man laughed. I wrapped my arms around myself as the men continued to ogle me.

"She is a member of our pack, and we protect our own." Max folded his arms over his chest. I stared at Max in surprise. They were defending me? Since when did Max and Easton protect me from anything?

"Well, this is different." Cora mused.

Easton leaned down and grabbed my backpack that I had dropped when the man had grabbed me.

The three men narrowed their eyes at Easton and Max, sizing them up. "Let me introduce myself." The lead guy said with a confident smile. "My name is Dax Wood, second son of the Alpha of the Morning Star Pack." His eyes returned to me. "Now, how about you come back over here, sweetheart, and we can finish what we started."

I blinked in surprise. Was he serious? Just because he was the son of an Alpha didn't mean I wanted anything to do with him. Easton moved, blocking Dax's view of me.

"Let us introduce ourselves. I'm Easton Shepherd, future Gamma of the Silver Moon Pack and this is Max Williams, our future Alpha."

"Like I said, we protect our own. And if I'm not mistaken, you three are trespassing on our land." Max pushed his aura out.

Mom had taught me to recognize high-ranking auras and to bow my head like other pack members would. Normal wolves couldn't help it, but for me, all the auras did was feel heavy. I thought about bowing before Max, but couldn't bring myself to do so. No one was looking at me anyway. The two goons next to Dax seemed to fight it, but eventually bowed their heads and bared their necks to Max while Dax only inclined his head. Easton even dipped his head slightly.

"I am going to have to ask you all to leave." Max growled out.

It was deathly still for several moments as the five men glared at one another. Finally, Dax and his guys turned and walked back into the forest. Before they disappeared, Dax looked back at me and winked. Cora scoffed and I scrunched my nose in disgust. That guy had way too much of an ego.

Once they were gone, I wrapped my arms around myself suddenly feeling cold. Easton and Max turned to look at me, but I kept my head down. It was best to stay quiet and eventually they would leave me alone. A hand touched my elbow and I jerked away.

Easton furrowed his eyebrows at my reaction to his touch. "Come on, let's get you home." He said kindly. He had never talked to me in such a soft way before. He only joked or taunted when speaking to me.

I eyed him warily before I shook my head and turned away from them. I began walking quickly, hoping they would leave me alone and go back to whatever they were doing before. We were halfway back to the pack residency district when I balled my hands into fists.

"Why are they still following me?" I growled.

"Maybe because they have your bag, and you are wearing Easton's shirt? Man, he is so freaking hot!" Cora threw out.

I looked down. I had forgotten Easton had put his shirt on me. I stopped and spun around to face Max and Easton. They stopped too and watched me.

"Can I have my bag back please?" I asked, totally expecting them to play keep away or something. They had done it before. But Easton handed it to me without hesitation.

I took off Easton's shirt and thrust it into his bare chest, causing the air to whoosh out of his lungs before digging my overly large hoodie out of my bag. I avoided their eyes as I slipped it on and put on my backpack. I turned and began walking again, only to stop a few minutes later when I heard them still following me. I spun around to face them, this time eyeing them suspiciously.

Max was wearing a plain t-shirt and Easton was pulling his on. They also had on swimming shorts, and flip flops. They had quite a bit more muscle now than before they left for camp, causing their shirts to pull tight across their chests and arms. They must have shifted. Werewolves, especially the males, tended to gain muscle quickly after they received their wolves.

Max's black hair was long enough that it curled over his ears and even though he probably shaved that morning, there was a shadow on his jaw. Easton had cut his hair. Instead of it being the same as Max's shaggy style, Easton's rich brown hair was short on the sides while the top was long enough to style. Both of them carried themselves with more confidence.

"I do have to say that the summer was good to them." Cora sighed and I inwardly rolled my eyes. *"Oh, come on Carr, you have to admit that Easton is really cute, especially with all those sculpted muscles we saw when he wasn't wearing his shirt."*

I ignored Cora as I crossed my arms over my chest. "Listen, I have had a very trying day and I don't need you two hanging around to make it worse, so please go away." Both Max and Easton's eyes went wide in surprise. *"What are the odds of us out running the future Gamma and future Alpha?"* I asked Cora, considering my options to get away.

"I say we have a fair shot, as long as they don't shift. You are in tennis shoes, and they are in flip flops." Cora said. *"If we can make it to the fork without them seeing us, then we can jump over the bush and onto the shelf just below the drop off. They will probably assume we took one of the forks."*

"Wow. Our little bookworm grew a spine while we were gone. I mean, I was a little impressed when you kneed Dax, but come on," Max gave a disbelieving laugh. "You haven't even given us a 'thank you' for saving you from those guys."

"A 'thank you' would imply I needed your help." I said before my eyes widened in shock.

I couldn't believe I had said that out loud. The shock on both Max and Easton's faces told me they were equally surprised. Cora, on the other hand, laughed hysterically. Having Cora to talk to freely, was starting to make it harder to hold my tongue when speaking with others.

Taking advantage of their surprise, I turned and sprinted down the path. I could hear them behind me, but they were falling behind fast. I increased my speed as I rounded the bend right before the fork and jumped the bush that separated the two paths. I almost missed the ledge. Teetering on the edge, I managed to throw my weight backward against the rock wall behind me instead of falling forward and down the twenty-foot drop.

Cora praised me for my skills at not dying just before I heard Max and Easton come to a stop right above me. My heart was pounding, and I prayed that they wouldn't hear it.

"Which way did she go?" Max panted.

"My guess is back to the housing district. We should follow her and make sure she gets home safely." Easton said breathlessly.

"Did you know that Carly was that tiny under all her oversized clothes?" Max laughed. "As much as I hate to agree with that Dax guy, she is definitely hot. How did we not notice before?" The sound of a growl followed by a phone notification filled the air. There was a moment of silence before Max sighed. "Alpha is requesting us back at the packhouse."

"We need to make sure Carly got home safe first. Those guys didn't look like they would give up easily." Easton's voice had a harder edge to it than a few minutes ago.

"I can't catch her scent. Your scent is mixing with hers and making it hard to know which way she went. She'll be fine. You can see her at the banquet. Everyone is going to be there." Max said. "And if she's not, we can sneak away and go to her house to check on her."

I glared at the drop off. What had gotten into them? They never cared about my safety. They had, on multiple occasions, stolen my coat and forced me to walk home in the dead of winter. Unlike normal juvenile werewolves, I was always cold. Not that they knew that, but still, who steals someone's coat when there is snow outside? Once I had even gotten sick from being out in the cold for too long. No, Easton and Max only cared about making me miserable.

I waited several minutes after Max and Easton's voices faded away before moving. I looked around, trying to find a good place to climb back up. Cora and I came to the same conclusion, I would have to climb up and through the bush. Unfortunately, the bush had long thick thorns. Taking a deep breath, I started to climb the rocky wall.

By the time I got back on the path, my hands were cut from the sharp rocks and because I was in shorts, I had deep scratches all over my legs. Thankfully, my hoodie protected my arms. I looked down at my watch and started jogging in the direction of the packhouse, ignoring the stinging on my legs. Thanks to my unexpected encounter with five egotistical males, I was going to be late for training with Gamma Jason.

It was a requirement that all seniors take a sparring class, but I demanded that the principal take it off my schedule. When the Alpha heard about it, he contacted my mother. They worked out a deal. I would still have to be in the sparring class, but I could do my homework instead if I did one-on-one lessons with Gamma Jason.

I started right after school let out for the summer and we have been meeting three times a week since. Now that school was starting, our schedule would need to change.

Gamma Jason had been surprised during our first several lessons. He had assumed I didn't know how to fight, but the opposite was true. I was an excellent fighter. My mother came from the North Wind Pack, which was filled with our kingdom's top fighters. The North Wind Pack supplied the Royal Pack with a lot of their guards and warriors. My parents had been two of the trainers there for a long time. Then something happened and my father was killed protecting me and mom.

We were forced to flee, and we took refuge with my aunt in a nearby pack. Mom grew worried that we weren't far enough away from the North Wind Pack, so we travelled for a while. We ended up joining the Silver Moon Pack.

Mom had been teaching me how to fight and defend myself from the time I could walk, and I hated it. Well, I didn't necessarily hate the art behind fighting, I just hated hurting others. That's why when it came to my bullies, I just kept quiet and stayed out of their way as best I could.

Gamma Jason had learned that I had many skills, but I just preferred not to use them. At first, he had been tough and unyielding, but as the summer went by, he began to see my resistance to fighting as an asset in a way. I had more patience than other wolves and that allowed me to have a clearer head during a fight. I took the time to study my opponent and learn their weaknesses. Most wolves just attacked and fought with brute strength.

He had been trying to convince me to reconsider joining the sparring class, but I was dead set against it. It hadn't taken long before he had softened to me and I to him. He had become like a father to me in many ways. It still baffled me that such a kindhearted man could be the father of the boy that had teased me since we were kids.

The packhouse came into view, and I slowed my pace as I approached the side door. I punched in the code and entered cautiously. I didn't want another run in with Max or Easton. I was still trying to understand the most recent one. They had been so protective.

I quickly moved down the hall and into the gym. Gamma Jason was already there talking with the very two people I had wanted to avoid. I slipped into the locker room before anyone could see me. I opened the door just a crack, so I could peek out and see what was going on. Max and Easton nodded at something Gamma Jason said before leaving.

When they were gone, I stepped back out and walked up to Gamma Jason with a smile. "What happened to you?" he asked as he looked at me with concern.

"I tripped and fell into a thorn bush." I shrugged as if it were no big deal.

"You're covered in blood, Carr. How did you end up falling in a thorn bush?" I looked down at myself. Sure enough, my legs had blood running from the multiple cuts and scratches. Gamma Jason grabbed my hands and I winced. My hands were worse than my legs. "And your hands? Carly, what happened?"

I slowly pulled my hands from his grasp. "I'm fine, really. It was an accident." I tried to soothe the man. "What's on the agenda for training?"

"Oh, um. No training today. Tonight is the banquet the pack is putting on for the returning high-ranking wolves. Easton just got home, and I want to catch up with him." My heart sank. If I wasn't training, mom would expect me to put on a dress and make an appearance at the banquet. "Sorry, I know how much you hate being in crowds, but I have to be there." Gamma Jason gave me an apologetic look. "Now go get yourself cleaned up. I will see you tonight."

"I understand." I said as I dropped my gaze to the floor. "See you later tonight." I mumbled before heading for the door.

Chapter 2

"Carly Brooks, you better be out here in two minutes!" Mom yelled up the stairs of our little house.

I looked at myself in the mirror and let out my breath slowly. Mom had bought me a new dress just for this occasion. It was a cream-colored, cap sleeved dress with a navy-blue lace overlay. The neckline was a V-neck that, thankfully, covered everything. I hated feeling exposed.

The dress hugged my figure nicely and the bow at the waist accentuated how tiny I was. The skirt flared out slightly and flowed down to my knees. Instead of the heels mom wanted me to wear, I had on my cowgirl boots. My long honey brown hair was curled, and I had applied a small amount of makeup that caused my blue eyes to pop.

"You have to admit, you look stunning." Cora told me.

"I do look nice." I admitted to her. The white popping through the blue lace gave the dress a very elegant look. I half turned to see the dress from a different angle. *"I just don't want to be noticed. If I am noticed, Marissa and her goons, or the torment triplets, will no doubt corner me somewhere. And I hate how exposed I feel in dresses."*

"That is why you are wearing shorts and a tank top underneath, so stop complaining. You are a vision." Cora laughed.

Mom came into my room without knocking and stopped just inside. Her smile was so big, and I felt guilty for all the hateful thoughts I had sent her way the whole time I had been getting ready. "You look beautiful, honey." Tears gathered in my mom's eyes. "You look just like…" Mom shook her head, and she quickly brushed the tears off her cheeks. She took a deep breath and smiled. "We are already late though, so we should get going."

Taking a deep breath for courage, I grabbed my leather jacket and followed my mom out the door. We walked the mile to the packhouse and stood in line to be admitted into the large banquet hall. The Alpha and Luna greeted us warmly as we entered.

There were already a ton of people and I felt like I was on display. There were several kids from school standing close to the door, and they were gawking at me. I really wished I had kept my jacket instead of turning it over to the Omega at the coat closet.

Someone called to Mom, and she quickly disappeared into the crowd, leaving me alone. I dropped my gaze to the floor so that my hair would shield my face before I moved slowly to the outskirts of the room. If I could find a dark corner, maybe I could hide out until it was time to go.

"Don't be so dramatic." Cora chastised. *"The only reason they are staring is because of how incredible you look. They have never seen you look like anything other than a pile of laundry before."*

"I like my hoodies, thank you very much." I muttered. "Plus, the whole idea is to go unnoticed. I don't want the attention." I told her as my eyes caught on two familiar faces.

Gamma Jason and his wife, Gamma Holly. Gamma Holly waved me over and I sighed in resignation as I made my way to them. Gamma Holly pulled me into a hug before stepping back to take a better look at me. "Carr, you look stunning." She gushed. "Doesn't she look amazing?" She turned to her husband and the three men standing beside him.

I stifled the groan that wanted to come out. Max, Easton, and the future Beta, Mike, were staring at me in complete shock. Easton's mouth hung open as he slowly took me in. "That she does, my dear." Gamma Jason beamed at me. I chose to ignore the three future leaders of the pack and smiled at Gamma Jason. "How are your injuries, Carr?"

"Injuries?" Gamma Holly gasped. She eyed me up and down again, her eyes settling on my gloved hands.

I wore gloves to hide the bandages that I put on my palms. "They are just fine." I smiled at him, but I could feel Easton and Max's gazes on me. "Like I told you earlier, sir, they are nothing."

"Hmm. Well at least your legs aren't bleeding anymore." Gamma Jason grumbled. "And I have told you to call me Jason."

"How did you get hurt?" Easton asked and my eyes darted in his direction. My heart skipped a beat before double timing to make up for it when our gazes locked.

"Carly said she tripped into a bush, but I don't buy it. She isn't clumsy." Gamma Jason informed the group.

"Of course, the bush." Max muttered under his breath. Music began to play, and he extended his hand to me. "Would you care to dance, Carly?" he asked with a smile.

I hesitated before grudgingly placing my hand in his. I bit the inside of my cheek as his hand closed over mine, causing the cuts on my palms to burn. He led me onto the dance floor and pulled me into his arms. I resisted the urge to run away.

"So, you jumped into a thorn bush to avoid me and East?" he asked, keeping his voice low so no one could overhear us.

"Wouldn't be the first time I went to extremes to avoid the two of you." I said, equally as quiet.

We danced without speaking for a long time. The song was coming to an end when Max spoke again. "We really aren't that bad, Carr." Max sounded almost offended.

I looked at him in disbelief. "You do realize you are talking to the girl you have teased relentlessly for over ten years, forced to walk three miles in the snow with no coat, and you have literally caused me to cry because of the things you have said." I glared at him. The song came to an end, and I pulled my hand out of his. "You, Mike, and Easton have done nothing but torment me since we were kids, so forgive me for not thinking you walk on water." I turned around and headed for the balcony doors. I needed air.

"I'm proud of you." Cora cheered me on. *"The look of surprise on his face will make sleeping at night so much easier. It's about time they realized what they have done to us."*

"I shouldn't have said anything." I muttered to myself in a quiet whisper.

"No, you should have." Max's voice was quiet, and I whirled around to see him standing a few feet behind me with his hands in his pockets.

"Should have what?" Easton walked out onto the balcony followed by Mike, and I glanced over the edge, gauging if I could jump without injuring myself. "You look like someone punched you in the gut, Max." Easton looked between us with a raised brow.

"The Torment Triplets." Cora said and I could feel both our defenses rise. *"If they start on you again, we should teach them a lesson."*

I dropped my gaze and clenched my hands together to stop them from shaking. *"No. I won't fight them if I can help it. They haven't physically hurt me before, and I don't think they will now."*

"Just another wakeup call." Max said quietly. "Are you cold, Carly? You're shaking." His voice was worried. He took a step towards me, and I took a step back, bumping into the rail. Max's expression changed from concern to one of hurt and understanding. "You are afraid of us." He said flatly.

I saw Easton's puzzled expression out of the corner of my eye. "I'm sorry, I shouldn't have said anything." I said as I glanced behind me. It was too far down. I would most likely break something if I tried.

"You were right, Carly. We were terrible to you. I'm sorry for everything we have done to you." My eyes snapped back to Max. "We teased you beyond what we should have." Max rubbed the back of his neck. "East, Mike, and I were complete jerks to you. While at training, we quickly realized that we were not on the top. Among other Alphas and high-ranking wolves, we were equals. To put it nicely, we were knocked down several pegs and I realized that the way I treat others matters." Max finally raised his eyes to meet mine. There was regret and pain there. "Please forgive me, Carly. I am trying to be a better man. Trying to be the leader this pack deserves."

I blinked in surprise. Cora huffed as she considered what Max had said. I didn't know what to say, so I glanced down. My hands were still shaking, but more from the cold than fear, now. I looked back up at him. "Look, I appreciate your apology, but I don't know if I can trust you." I said softly.

"Carly, please..."

"Max, we did a lot of damage to Carly." East said softly and I looked at him. He watched me with a pained expression. "I am sorry too. I was drawn to you, and your silent acceptance of our teasing made it easy for me to keep seeking you out. Everyone else reacted too quickly, which made it less fun. It had become a game to try to get you to react. I was cruel to you, and I am sorry." Easton took a step closer. I didn't move; too stunned to do anything.

I closed my eyes as years and years of their teasing and harassment flooded my mind. If I had just yelled at them, would they have left me alone? I looked back at Easton as a tear fell on my cheek. "You made me cry." I snapped and he flinched. "You stole my jacket and I had to walk home in the snow." My hands fisted as my frustration grew. "I was sick for a week, Easton. A week of a fever and chills and coughing."

"You got sick? You are a werewolf; we don't get sick." Max said, confused.

I glared at him. "Congratulations. You have met your first werewolf that feels cold constantly and gets sick and it takes me longer to heal." I took a threatening step towards them. "You three made it so that I was afraid to go to school. I would hear you coming and hide. I nearly fell off a cliff trying to avoid you today." All three of their eyes widened in surprise. "I don't heal like other wolves. I get sick. I don't like to fight. I hate attention and I do not want to be here." I stormed past them and back into the crowded room.

"You go, girl!" Cora cheered in my head.

I wrapped my arms around myself as I headed for the exit. The entrance hall was crowded, so I took the side hall that led towards the gym. I pushed open the side door and took a breath of the cool night air. The balcony had felt stifling with Easton, Mike, and Max there. Tears fell down my cheeks as I slowly followed the path that led back home.

"What did I do?" I asked Cora. *"I can't believe I unloaded on them like that. I should have kept my mouth shut."*

"Even though they seemed penitent, they still needed to know that their actions had consequences." Cora said softly.

"But I told them about my weaknesses. Now they will use that against me." I sighed as my hand brushed the bracelet on my opposite wrist.

The bracelet matched my mother's. They masked our scent and helped hide us from the North Wind Pack. The downside was that it made me weak, like a human. It could even make it harder for me to find my mate when I turned eighteen. Mom didn't have the same problem with getting sick. She was just as healthy and strong as ever. The only thing we could think of to explain it was I hadn't shifted yet.

"Carly, wait!" Easton's voice called and I stopped. What did he want? I wiped my cheeks as I turned around. I wasn't going to give him another reason to tease me. He stopped a few feet away.

"What do you want, Easton?" I sighed tiredly.

He moved nervously. "You didn't grab your jacket." He said, handing it to me. I stared at it confused for a moment before slowly taking it from him. "I'm sorry, Carly. I truly am. I had no idea." His voice trailed off as he shook his head. "Not that that is an excuse." He took a deep breath before continuing. "I know I have hurt you. You have every right to hate me. But please, I'm trying to do better, be better. I know it will take a while to earn back any amount of your trust, but I am willing to put forth the effort. Please forgive me."

A laugh farther down the path caused me to step closer to Easton as I turned to see who had joined us. I was still not happy with Easton, but he was better than an unknown threat.

"Well, sweetheart, it seems your mate has landed himself in your black book. Why don't you come with me, and I can show you what a real man is like?" Dax's voice caused me to shiver in disgust.

Easton took a protective step forward, shielding me from the approaching man. "What are you doing here?" He growled.

"We were invited to the party. We were on our way there when we heard you begging for forgiveness. Such a weak thing to do." Dax tsked.

We? I glanced around and noticed at least seven men around us. I touched Easton's back as I stepped closer to him, and he glanced at me. His jaw tightened before turning his attention back to Dax. I could feel the tension rolling off of Easton as we stood there. He was gearing up for a fight. I could feel it. I needed to deescalate the situation.

"I am not your sweetheart, Mr. Wood. The party is not far, just continue down this path and you will find the packhouse. I'm sure Alpha Callum is anticipating your arrival." I said sweetly.

"As a gentleman, I can't leave you alone with someone you are arguing with." Dax smiled back.

"That is where you are wrong." I said, stepping even closer to Easton. He grabbed my hand and warmth spread through me. Calmness took over the anxiety building in me, giving me a confidence I normally didn't have. "My relationship with someone has nothing to do with you. I do not require your assistance now or ever."

"What if I were to tell you that I am your mate and seeing you with another man is not working for me?" Dax said, stepping forward and Easton's grip on my hand tightened.

I didn't even hesitate. "I am calling your bluff. You have commented multiple times that you think Easton and I are mates, which makes your recent claim seem manipulative." I tugged on Easton's hand as I continued down the path towards my house. Dax's men let us pass, but Dax held his ground.

"You are making a mistake she-wolf." Dax's voice held a warning. "Why are you settling for a mere Gamma instead of aligning yourself with an Alpha?"

I released Easton's hand as I stepped up to Dax. A triumphant smile spread on his face as he put a hand on my cheek. "Get out of my way before we have a repeat of what happened earlier." I said quietly so only he could hear me.

He raised his brow in surprise and his hand slipped down to my neck. "Are you threatening me?" His hand tightened ever so slightly, and Cora growled. I resisted the urge to panic. I had no doubt that he wanted to squeeze harder, but was holding himself back.

"Of course not." I said as I slapped his hand away from me and shouldered past him. "I would never threaten anyone. That was just a warning." I looked back over my shoulder. Easton was close to my side with a look of confusion and amusement. "If you touch me again, if you look at me like I am some sort of buffet, I will make sure you don't forget what happens when you disrespect a woman." I growled out.

Easton wrapped his arm around my waist as we began walking away from the group of men. As soon as we were out of earshot he began to laugh. "I had no idea you had such a feisty side." He smiled down at me. "For someone who claims to not like to fight, you almost picked one with nearly fifteen grown werewolves."

Unconsciously, I leaned into Easton as we walked. My earlier fight had left me, and I shivered. He pulled me closer to his side and I stopped walking. I looked up at him as my brain registered that he was still holding me. I took a step away from him, putting a good amount of distance between us.

"I am still mad at you." I said as I dropped my gaze to the ground.

"I know." He sighed. "Let's get you home so you don't freeze."

"You don't have to..." I started to say but he grabbed my hand and pulled me after him.

"I think I do. The look in Dax's eyes as he looked at you...Yeah, I'm walking you home." Easton kept hold of my hand as he increased his speed. He was practically dragging me down the path. I tripped and he caught me. After that he slowed a bit, but he continued to walk quickly. He finally released me when we got to my house. "I'll wait here until you get inside." He said, scanning our surroundings.

I tried to turn the door handle, but it was locked. I let out a frustrated sigh as I looked back at Easton. "My mom has the keys." I said before looking back at the house. I remembered cracking my window while I was getting ready. I stepped off the porch and started to walk around the side of the house.

"Where are you going?" Easton asked as he followed me.

"I am going to my room. You can go back to your party now." I answered without looking at him.

I stopped below my window. There was no lattice, no vines, and no way up. Except for me. I was small for a werewolf. I was barely five foot five, while most girls were closer to five foot ten. My lighter frame made climbing easier, and Mom had insisted I learned to free climb, just in case.

Luckily for me, I had on my workout shorts still and an undershirt under my dress. I reached around my back to try to unzip my dress but couldn't quite reach it.

"What are you doing?" Easton asked anxiously.

I turned to face him, annoyed that he was still there and also grateful that I wouldn't have to ruin my dress by climbing in it. I debated if I should trust Easton. Something inside me told me I could.

"Just unzip this dress, will you?" I said as I turned my back to him and moved my hair out of the way.

There was a moment where nothing happened, then I felt his fingers graze my neck as he grasped the zipper. A tingling sensation spread across my skin where his fingers touched. When he finished, I turned to look at him. He cleared his throat as he turned away from me.

"Don't look." I said firmly, testing to see if he would peek or not.

"Seriously, what are you doing?" He asked while keeping his back towards me. "How is undressing going to get you inside?"

"I am going to climb up to my window." I said and he turned his head to look at the side of the house. I pulled my gloves off and dropped them on the ground. "I'm going to hand you my dress so you can take it to the front. My mom will kill me if anything happens to it."

"Carly, I hate to be the bearer of bad news, but there is no way up the side of the house." Easton's voice held skepticism.

"Easton?" He glanced over at me. My dress was still fully on, but I could still see a slight pinking on his cheeks in the moonlight. "I am willing to bet that I can make it up to my window."

He chuckled as he turned his back. "What do you get if you make it up there?"

I slipped the dress off, careful to keep it from touching the ground. "Hmm. You, Mike, and Max have to do something for me, no matter what it is."

"And if you don't make it?" Easton asked with a smile in his voice. I stepped closer to him.

"You can't get this dress dirty at all. Mom literally threatened to kill me if I ruined it." I said as I stepped around him and handed him my dress. He took it and then looked at me. His eyebrows rose in surprise.

"What? You thought I was really going to trust you enough to undress with you here?"

He smiled and a dimple appeared. Butterflies fluttered in my stomach. "So, what do I get if I win?"

"I forgive you three without holding anything over your heads. We start clean." I suggested.

He shifted his weight as he looked back at the house. "I don't like this. You could really get hurt."

I shivered as the breeze blew, and he stepped closer. He was still a foot from me, but I could easily feel his warmth. What would it be like to produce so much heat and not be bothered by the cold? "It's not your choice, Easton. It's mine." I said as I slipped my boots and socks off before turning to the house. "Meet you at the front door."

I gripped the brick that I knew had a good hand hold and began my ascent. It was slow going and I picked each hold with care. My foot slipped once which caused my hands to burn, but I managed to recover. I finally reached the window. I took a breath and let go with my right hand and tore the screen off. It crashed to the ground, and I could hear the rumbling of a male voice speaking quietly below me but I didn't dare glance down. I pushed the window up enough for me to slip in.

I pulled my body through the window and hit the floor hard. I let out a laugh as I rolled to my feet and leaned out the window with a triumphant smile. Two shadowy figures stood there. When they saw me, they moved towards the front of the house.

"Who's with Easton?" I asked Cora as I headed for my bedroom door.

"Beats me." Cora was just as confused as I was.

I opened the front door to find Easton and Max standing there. I don't know why I was even surprised to see Max there, but I was. I opened the door all the way and motioned for them to enter.

"How did you…?" Easton shook his head as he stepped inside. "That was insane."

"Thanks." I said slowly as I reached to take my boots from Max. Blood was soaking through the bandages I had put on earlier. "Shoot." I said as I ran to the kitchen sink. I turned on the faucet and unwrapped my hands, sticking them in the warm water. "You can set my boots by the couch and the dress you can drape over one of the chairs at the table." I said as I rinsed the grime that had gotten into the bandages from climbing, out of the cuts.

"How did you hurt your hands?" East asked as he stepped up to my side.

"Climbing." I glanced over at him before turning the water off and grabbing the paper towels.

"Those don't look like cuts you get from a brick wall where there aren't hand holds." Max came up on my other side.

Easton reached for my hands and took over patting them dry. His hands were warm and oddly comforting. "Where is your first aid kit?" he asked as the cuts continued to bleed.

I sighed. "Upstairs, hall closet."

Easton sent Max a look. "On it." Max said as he ran up the stairs.

"I can do this." I tried to protest, but the look Easton gave me had me closing my mouth.

"He looks mad." Cora observed. *"Why is he mad?"*

I tried to pull my hands away, but Easton's growl stopped me. Max came back down with the large first-aid box and set it on the table. The pressure Easton was putting on my hands hurt. Even my whimper of pain didn't make his grip loosen. He pulled me over to the table and pushed me down into a chair. Max and Easton began pulling items out of the kit and dressing my injuries. They didn't talk to me, but they communicated with each other, which was irritating.

When they were done, I was glaring at them. Max grabbed my elbow and dragged me over to the couch. He gave me a gentle shove, causing me to fall back onto the couch.

"What the heck?" I snapped.

"How did you hurt your hands? The truth this time." Easton growled.

"I told you the truth. I hurt them climbing." I watched as both men crossed their arms over their chests as they glared at me. They were definitely an intimidating pair.

Silence stretched on as we glared at each other. After several minutes, I huffed as I stood. I began pacing as I tried to control my anger. I needed to go for a run to blow off some steam, but I doubted Max and Easton would allow me to grab my running shoes.

"Maybe you should just tell them all the details." Cora suggested. *"Their recent behavior makes me think they would feel bad and leave us alone."*

"I shouldn't have to tell them anything." I snapped at her. *"It's not like they are my Alpha or Gamma."*

"They may be a little more humble because they got a taste of their own medicine at camp, but they are still as high headed as before."

I glared over at them as I continued to pace. They wore matching expressions that told me they weren't going to drop this. "Why? Why do you even care?" I yelled. "You have never cared about me before. You can't just come in here and demand answers from me." I fumed as I paced. "Cora is right, you two are just like you have always been." I muttered to myself.

"Who is Cora? I don't recognize the name." Max asked. "Was she with you when you got hurt?"

I laughed. Of course, Cora had been with me. I stopped my pacing and looked over at Easton and Max. They were watching me expectantly. I had mentioned Cora to them. I swallowed nervously. "I jumped the thorn bush at the fork this afternoon to avoid you two." I said quickly.

"The one that is at the start of the crevasse at the fork?" Easton asked with wide eyes.

"There is a shelf about five feet down just below the bush. I was there when you guys made it to the fork. After you left, I had to climb back out. The rock is sharp there." I said as I plopped back on the couch. "My hands got cut by the rocks, my legs by the bush."

"If you had missed that shelf, you could have been seriously injured." Max's eyes were wide in surprise. "Are you really that afraid of us that you would risk that?"

"Do I need to give you a copy of ten years' worth of diary entries?" I asked as I rolled my eyes.

"How does this, Cora, fit into all this?" Easton asked.

I stared at him. I had hoped my confession about the fork would distract them from Cora. "Cora isn't what's important here." I said flatly.

"Hey!" Cora protested.

"Sorry. You know that you are important. I just cannot let them know about you yet." I told her.

"You are right. What is important is the fact that you jumped off a cliff to avoid us." Easton snapped.

I stood back up and took a step towards him, eyes blazing. "You walked me home, I'm inside, you can leave now." I growled. He blinked in surprise at my show of aggression.

"Come on, Carly. Let's all take a deep breath and discuss this calmly." Max grabbed my arm and pulled me back a step. I shook him off.

"We have already talked about this. You two teased and tormented me to the point that I altered my daily routines and hid myself from everyone. Now you come back after three months claiming to have changed, all because you got a taste of your own medicine. You expect me to just forget the past ten years and put my faith and trust in you?" I moved to the front door and yanked it open. "I want both of you to leave." I glared at them until they hesitantly moved to the door. Max stepped out first and waited on the porch. Easton paused in front of me, and I dropped my gaze as tears burned my eyes. I knew he saw them because he looked concerned, and his jaw tightened.

He reached a hand towards me, but I shook my head and stepped back. He ran a hand through his hair as he stepped onto the porch. He turned back to look at me and I slammed the door in his face and locked it.

I ran upstairs and pulled on my running shoes before unfolding my treadmill that was next to my window. As I stepped onto the belt, I saw two shadows not far off. Easton and Max. I wasn't going to cry this time. I was going to run until the desire to scream and cry went away. Cora disagreed with me. She wanted to hunt them down and plant them each a facer, which made me laugh. I plugged my earphones in and ran.

Chapter 3

It had been a full two weeks since the night of the banquet. I had managed to avoid both Easton and Max, which was difficult because they were back at the school. School had started two days after their return and Alpha Callum had assigned the future Alpha, Beta, and Gamma, teaching positions.

Max was team-teaching war strategy with last year's instructor. I didn't need to take that class, thank goodness. Mike taught gym class for the lower grades, and I occasionally saw him when he left the gym as I headed in for sparring class. He didn't mess with me, but he always paused and watched me. Easton was harder to avoid. He taught the men's sparring class. The boys' class was held in the wrestling room which was right next to the gym where the girls' class was held.

I adjusted my backpack as I headed for my usual spot against the wall. Sparring class would be starting soon and the other she-wolves were filtering into the gym. I dropped my bag on the floor just before I was slammed into the brick wall. I spun around to see Marissa's smirking face.

"Oh, I'm sorry. I didn't see you there." She sneered. I dropped my gaze and prayed she would move on. Luck wasn't on my side today and she grabbed my jaw, yanking my head up to look at her. "You are no better than a human, slow and weak. Why don't you go live with them. Maybe they would want you, Runt." She punched me in the stomach, and I sucked in a quick breath. She didn't give me time to recover before delivering another blow.

"Stop letting her hit you, Carly. This is unacceptable." Cora yelled.

"What is going on here?" Easton's angry voice caused the gym to go quiet. Marissa let go of me as she spun around to face him with a sweet smile.

I pressed my hand to my stomach as I slowly straightened. "There will be no fighting in my class unless you are on the mats." He glared at us.

"We were just messing around, Easton. Nothing to worry about. Where's Gamma Holly?" Marissa asked as she took several steps in Easton's direction. She was batting her eyelashes at him with a flirtatious smile on her lips. She grabbed his arm and I looked away.

"Gamma Holly is needed on a project for the next couple of days. We are combining the boys' and girls' classes for the meantime." Easton explained, turning his attention to the whole gym as he shook off her hand and ignored her attempt to flirt. I glanced around and noticed that the boys were on the other side of the room. "Pair up and we will begin." Easton called out as he walked away.

People started to pair up and I lowered myself to the ground. I pulled out my textbook and turned to today's homework assignment. Not five minutes later, I felt a presence hovering close by. I looked up to find Easton watching me with irritation in his expression. "Can I help you?" I asked, setting down my pencil.

"Get on the mats." He ordered.

"Excuse me?" I narrowed my eyes. I didn't spar here.

"You heard me." He reached down and grabbed my arm and lifted me to my feet, causing my book to fall to the floor. "You are in a sparring class; you are going to spar like everyone else."

"I don't fight." I stammered as he dragged me to the mats. I hated that his touch caused my heartbeat to quicken.

He ignored me and shoved me onto a mat. I looked at the other people around me. All the she-wolves were watching with wide eyes. They all knew I didn't fight. Marissa was the only one who looked gleeful. "I'll spar with her." She volunteered eagerly.

"Of course she would want to spar with us." Cora rolled her eyes. *"Thanks to you refusing to fight back, she thinks we are weak."*

I looked around helplessly as panic started to fill me. "Get in your fighting stance." Easton ordered. I glared over at him. Oh, I was going to kill him. He was trying to get me to react, but I wouldn't play his game. "Get. In. Your. Fighting. Stance." He said again, this time more slowly. I turned to face Marissa. She had her guard up and she looked way too excited. I swallowed down my apprehension.

"I'm going to let her win." I told Cora. *"I'm not fighting."*

"But this girl is a terrible person." Cora argued. *"We could take this time to teach her a lesson."*

"Winning isn't going to solve our Marissa problem." I glanced back in Easton's direction. *"It will make it worse. I'm sorry, Cora, but this is going to hurt."*

"She is close to shifting. I can sense it." Cora warned. *"That will make her more aggressive."*

I raised my guard slowly. In my peripheral vision, I saw the whole class gathering around to watch. It wasn't going to be much of a show. I wasn't going to fight.

"Fight!" Easton called.

Marissa advanced quickly and I dropped my guard. I barely registered Easton yelling for us to stop before Marissa delivered several quick blows to my face and stomach. I dropped to my knees, and she jumped on my back, knocking me onto my stomach. Marissa pinned my arms under her legs and wrapped her arm around my neck.

I took a deep breath just before my oxygen was cut off. I didn't struggle because I knew someone would stop her from killing me. I heard far away yelling as my vision went black.

*   *   *

"Were you even going to let her go?" A male voice yelled. "I told you to stop several times before that. That's not how this class is going to be run. When I say to stop, you stop!"

"I'm sorry, sir." Marissa said innocently. "She didn't tap. How was I supposed to know to let her go?"

"You are supposed to be aware of your opponent. You could have killed her. Not to mention the fact that I told you to stop before the first strike." Easton snapped. "You can report to the principal's office. I will not have you in this class if you are a danger to the other students."

"But…" Marissa started to say, but a threatening growl cut her off.

I coughed and blinked my eyes open. The voices in the gym went quiet and a hand touched my face. Warmth spread through me as my vision came into focus. Easton was kneeling beside me. "Are you okay?" he asked, concern lacing his voice.

I shoved his hand away as I scooted backwards. His brows drew down in confusion. "I told you I don't fight." I snapped at him as I got to my feet.

My vision tilted slightly, and I shook my head to clear it as I stumbled over to my bag. I picked up my textbook and slammed it closed before shoving it into my backpack.

"You are in a sparring class, Carly. You have to fight." Easton said as he followed me.

I whirled around to face him. "No. No, I don't. Every time you put me on the mats the same thing is going to happen, because I will not fight!" I yelled.

I turned towards the gym doors and left. I didn't slow down, even when I heard Easton calling after me, and as soon as I got outside, I ran. I headed in the direction of my house and then changed my mind.

The packhouse was quiet with most of the juvenile wolves still at school. I slipped through the side door and into the gym without seeing anyone.

I changed in the locker room and went to the treadmill. I still had just over an hour before I was supposed to meet Gamma Jason, and I planned on making the most of it, even with my muscle screaming in protest from my fight with Marissa. I put my earphones in, turned up my music, and ran.

A tap on my shoulder pulled me out of my angry thoughts. I glanced over to find Alpha Callum and Gamma Jason standing there. I pushed the stop button and let the machine slow to a stop before pulling out my earphones.

"The school called." Gamma Jason stated. I sighed and stepped off the machine and grabbed a bottle of water out of the mini fridge in the corner. "Sparring class seemed to be eventful."

"If you say so." I said quietly.

"I heard that you left school early following an incident where a student was knocked unconscious." Gamma Jason commented. "Easton said he would give a full report when he gets here after the school day is over."

I turned around to face the Alpha and Gamma and waited for them to continue. If they were going to punish me for leaving school early, then so be it.

"We just wanted to make sure you were okay." Alpha Callum looked me over, but I didn't react. "I have a meeting with Marissa and her parents in a few minutes to get her side of the story. Once Easton gives his report, we will meet with you and your mother."

"Understood, sir." I said, keeping my eyes lowered.

"Are you still up to training?" Gamma Jason asked, and my head snapped up.

"Yes, sir." I was confused as to why he would ask such a thing. He was the one always pushing me to train more.

He nodded and motioned for me to follow him to the sparring room. The room was a huge open area with padded mats on the floor and the lower part of the walls. Jason turned on the stereo, blasting our favorite workout music before we stepped out on the mats. We immediately got into training.

We had been in the gym for thirty minutes. Jason grabbed me around my waist, pinning me to him before getting his arm around my neck and squeezing. I twisted and broke his hold before knocking him off balance and putting him in an arm bar. He tapped out and the music was turned off and someone started clapping.

I looked around to see Alpha Callum, my mom, Gamma Holly, and Easton standing there. Mom was the one clapping and beaming with pride while the others looked on in surprise.

"Well done, sweetheart." Mom called. "Interesting choice to go with the arm bar."

"Thanks, mom." I said quietly as I glanced between those gathered. I was breathing hard, and I was all sweaty.

"I thought you said you couldn't fight." Easton accused.

I shook my head. "I said I *didn't* fight, not that I *couldn't*." I corrected as I glared at him.

"Carly, hun, what happened to your face?" Mom's eyes blazed with fury as she turned them to Jason. "You said you wouldn't actually strike her with enough force to leave a mark."

"Gamma Jason didn't do this, mom." I said as I sighed. "It was a misunderstanding at school. Don't worry about it."

Alpha Callum raised his brows in surprise, but it was Easton who spoke. "A misunderstanding? You dropped your guard the moment the match began. You didn't even move a muscle to defend yourself. You let her hit you and then choke you out." Easton said through clenched teeth. "Why?"

My eyes met his and I wanted to punch him in the face. "I told you I didn't like to fight, Easton. You were the one who pushed me on the mat. You were the one who wanted to see the fight." I snapped at him. "I have an arrangement with Alpha Callum, Gamma Holly, and Gamma Jason."

Gamma Jason grabbed my arm to hold me back. I hadn't realized I was moving towards Easton. "If you want to take out your frustration, do it on the mats." he stated, motioning behind us.

I glanced at Easton who moved to the mats. I debated as I watched him move to the center of the room. I followed him, stopping several feet away.

"I'm not going to fight you, Easton." I glared at him.

"Why not? I know you want to hit me." He threw his arms out to either side, giving me a free shot.

"Because you want me to!" I yelled back. "I don't like to fight." I said slowly. "Just because I want to hit you doesn't mean I will. It's called self-control. Maybe you should try it sometime." I turned and walked away. "Is training done for the day?" I asked Gamma Jason.

"Training is over, but something needs to be done about the attack that happened in class." Alpha Callum said. "According to Easton and several students, Marissa pinned your arms down so you couldn't tap out. That kind of aggression is unacceptable."

"She is turning eighteen in a day or two. It is probably just her wolf trying to come out. Don't juvenile wolves become more aggressive before a shift?" I asked. Marissa was mean and she often went out of her way to hurt me in some way, but this time had been excessive.

"Your face is bruised, and she nearly killed you, yet you don't want me to do anything?" Alpha Callum asked, confused.

"Carly, this is serious." Gamma Holly said. "This isn't the only time she has singled you out. Last year…"

"I understand Gamma Holly. If you and Alpha feel the need to punish her for her actions, I understand, but I will not be a part of it. Excuse me." I said as I left the sparring gym. I could hear mom and Gamma Jason entering the conversation before the door closed behind me.

I reentered the gym, but before I reached the locker room, the gym door opened again. "What do you want?" I asked, knowing it was Easton that had followed me.

"Carly, I'm sorry I forced you to spar when you had obviously been against it. I should have never done that, especially with the girl that was attacking you at the beginning of class." I spun around to face Easton, my hands in fists. "I just thought if you could work it out on the mats, things would be better for you."

"You know nothing about girls, do you?" I laughed and shook my head. "Guys can beat each other up over something and by the end of the fight there are no hard feelings. Girls are not like that. They fight and they hold grudges. Marissa will now be worse than ever because she won the fight."

"Then why did you let her win?" he asked, confused. "You are obviously the better fighter."

"Because if I had won, she would have tried again and again until she did win." I threw my hands in the air as I turned around to try to escape into the locker room, but Easton grabbed my arm to stop me. Warmth spread through me again and my anger started to cool.

"I'm sorry, okay?" he said desperately as he turned me to face him. "I was just trying to help." His eyes scanned over my face and guilt filled his expression. "Why didn't you defend yourself?" He whispered as he raised his other hand and ran a finger along my tender jaw.

"Is my face really that bad?" I asked with a raised brow. Easton let out a tense laugh and dropped his hand from my cheek.

"You aren't horrible to look at, even with the bruising, if that is what you're asking?" Easton scanned my face again with a small smile. His eyes settled on my lips for several seconds before raising back to my eyes.

"Okay, I think I'm starting to like this guy." Cora drooled. *"Not only is he attractive, but he is also proving to be protective, and he thinks we are pretty, even when we are sporting a black eye."*

"Really, Cora? That's how it's going to be?" I asked her. "You do remember he was the one that teased me for years and was the one who started the fight?"

"But he is apologizing." Cora sighed.

I looked into his amazing green eyes and wondered if I could really forgive him for the past ten years. "Can I ask you something?" I asked softly.

Easton moved a little closer, his natural body heat warmed me and made me want to lean into him, but I resisted the urge. "Sure." His voice was slightly deeper.

"Are you ready to pay up for losing our bet?" I asked and his brow quirked up. His dimple appeared as a smile slowly spread on his lips.

"What did you have in mind?" Easton's voice took on a flirtatious edge as his eyes flick down to my lips again.

I smiled sweetly at him and his eyes darkened. "I need you and Max to convince both of your parents to lessen Marissa's punishment."

Easton's crooked grin turned into a scowl. "No." he said firmly, taking a step away. "She hurt you, Carly. I cannot allow that." He growled before storming out of the gym.

I blinked in surprise at his sudden departure. *"What was that about?"* I asked Cora.

"I have no idea." Cora mused.

I went into the locker room and collected my things. I didn't bother changing before I left, intending on taking a nice warm shower once I got home. As I walked towards the path that led back to the residency district, I felt eyes watching me. I glanced around to see if I could spot whoever it was.

Standing near a car, Easton was glaring at me while Max looked ready to laugh. His eyes narrowed on me. When I turned to fully face them, his eyes went wide. Max's face hardened the moment he saw my bruises.

I turned my back to them and walked away. I didn't want to get into it again with the two of them. I could feel them watching me until the path curved into the forest.

Chapter 4

    I was snuggled under a blanket as I sat on the couch in the front room. The TV was on as background noise while I worked on my homework. I had been taking extra classes throughout the summer and accelerated classes during the school year in order to graduate half a year early. So far, I was right on track. Even though the year was only a quarter of the way through, I was preparing for midterms. Not very many people knew that I was graduating early. Other than my teachers, only the Alpha, the principal, and mom knew.

    I needed to get my studying done now while I could, because in a few short hours, I had to be at the trial for Marissa. The incident happened a couple of weeks ago, but the trial kept getting pushed back. Marissa had been moved into a different sparring class in the meantime. I didn't need to worry about avoiding Easton, because he was doing a good enough job avoiding me.

    I had spotted him a few times in the halls, but he would walk the other way. There were times that I felt like I was being watched. I would spot Mike, Max or Easton and instead of feeling creeped out, I had the odd sensation of being protected.

    A knock on the front door pulled me from my thoughts. I set my book down before getting up and answering the door. Easton stood on the porch with his hands in his pockets. He was dressed in black slacks, a dark green dress shirt that set off his eyes, a black tie and a black blazer that was tailored to him. I swallowed hard. Easton looked like he stepped out of a catalog.

    He looked me up and down, the corner of his lips twitching. "Is that what you are wearing to the trial?" He asked.

    I glanced down at my sweatpants and hoodie as my hand moved to the messy bun on top of my head. I quickly looked at my watch. "Oh no." I muttered as I sprinted up the stairs. "Make yourself at home." I yelled before slamming my bedroom door.

I grabbed a black pencil skirt and dark blue button-down blouse. I did the bare minimum amount of makeup before brushing my hair and pulling it into a high ponytail. Grabbing the heels my mom insisted I wear; I raced down the stairs. Easton stood as I entered the living room. His eyes took me in, and he smiled.

"What?" I asked breathlessly as I tucked in my shirt.

"Nothing. Just you were only up there for like ten minutes." Easton gave me another once over. "I'm just amazed you went from drowning in your baggy clothes to this in such a short time."

"Thanks." I narrowed my eyes at him. "Wait. Why are you here? Mom was supposed to come get me when it was time." I used the wall to balance as I slipped my heels on.

"Dad sent me to get you. Something about them needing to interview your mom before the trial begins." Easton shrugged, but his eyes remained fixed on me.

I checked my appearance in the hall mirror quickly before opening the front door and stepping out onto the porch. It was overcast and I could smell rain. I paused as I looked at the sky. I really hoped it didn't rain. Easton offered me his hand to help me down the stairs and I slipped my hand into his. Warmth spread up my arm at the contact. He let go as soon as I was on solid ground, but the sensation of his hand wrapped around mine persisted, even though we were no longer touching.

"I hate heels." I muttered once we were walking towards the packhouse.

Easton laughed. "If you hate them, why are you wearing them?"

"Mom insisted on it." I said as if that explained everything. I shivered as the wind picked up. The temperature was definitely dropping with the approaching storm. Easton shrugged out of his blazer and draped it around my shoulders. I gratefully slid my arms into the sleeves before wrapping my arms around myself. "Thanks. I forgot my jacket on my bed."

"No problem." He smiled at me before returning his attention straight ahead. "It amazes me that you were in sweatpants, that ridiculously oversized hoodie, and a blanket. Do you ever feel warm?"

"Not usually." I shrugged. "I've always been cold. I get sick easily because of it."

"Your boyfriend probably enjoys that about you." He glanced over at me. "That way you are always up for cuddling."

I laughed. Boyfriend? "What makes you think I have a boyfriend?" I asked, smiling.

"You would have to be okay with getting attention in order to have a boyfriend." Cora laughed as well.

"You are always wearing a guy's sweatshirt, your scent isn't quite right, almost like it is mixed with something else, and you don't give any guy at school the time of day." Easton glanced at me again.

His reasonings made me laugh harder. "The hoodies belonged to my dad before he died. I don't know what you mean about my scent. And none of the guys at school are my type." I addressed each of his observations. "My own personal heater does sound nice though." I sighed. We fell into a comfortable silence as we walked.

The packhouse came into view a few minutes later and my stomach knotted with anxiety. My steps began to slow. Easton put a hand on my lower back to keep me moving forward.

As we entered the main hall, Max stood there leaning against a pillar. When he saw us he straightened to his full height. "Good, you got her." He said in way of greeting.

"I didn't think I was that late." I said quietly as I lowered my gaze to the floor.

"You aren't. They are just wanting to get this over with." Max grabbed my arm and pulled me to the door.

I looked back at Easton, anxiety filling me again. He was still standing in the center of the entry hall watching me. When our gazes connected, he gave me a small smile and nod. I wanted to run back to him, where I knew I would be safe, but Max opened the door and gave me a gentle nudge into the room. "Good luck." He said before closing the door between us and I was left standing there alone.

I stared at the door in shock. What had come over me? Why had I wanted to run to Easton? The need to be close to him was overwhelming and I shook my head trying to shake the feeling. It had to be the crazy amount of stress I was under with this trial.

A throat cleared and I looked over my shoulder to find three people sitting behind a long table watching me. Three rows of seating stretched from one side of the room to the other, with an aisle in the center. I was at one end of the aisle which led to an open area in front of the long table. There was a circle on the ground where one stood when being asked questions.

The man that sat in the middle had short grey hair and a weathered face. He beckoned me forward. I slowly walked toward them until I stood in the circle. I wrung my hands nervously as I stared at the floor.

"State your name for the record." The man's voice was deep and carried a bored tone.

I swallowed. "Carly Brooks."

"Carly, do you know why you are here?" The woman to his left asked. I looked up at her. She had a kind face and long straight silvery hair that hung down around her shoulders.

"Not entirely, ma'am." I said softly.

"As members of this pack's counsel, it is our job to help keep order among the pack members. Alpha Callum has asked us to take over this case because he felt too involved in the situation." She said softly with a smile.

"Councilwoman Georgia is correct. We are to decide the consequences of this attack." The man in the center said.

I glanced over at the man on the right. He was watching me closely as if he were trying to puzzle something out. He was younger than the other two council members. He had black hair and a thick black beard with piercing blue eyes.

"This is Councilman Borus and Counselman Jet. We will be asking you some questions to clarify the events of the attack on you." Councilwoman Georgia said kindly as she pointed to the man in the middle and then the man at the end of the table. I nodded my head in understanding and waited.

"The girl that attacked you is Marissa Hampton?" Counselman Borus asked as he looked down at a paper in front of him. He was bored and didn't appear to even care about the outcome.

"I thought this was when we got to tell our side of the story. Sounds like they have already made up their minds about what happened." Cora pointed out.

"The girl I was sparring with was Marissa Hampton." I clarified. Borus looked at me with a raised brow.

"You are claiming Marissa Hampton did not attack you?" Jet asked, leaning forward.

"The way you are implying 'attack' suggests Marissa came after me without me knowing she would. That would be incorrect. We were sparring partners, and from my understanding, sparring involves attacking one's partner." I said looking Jet straight in the eye.

"We have talked with Alpha Callum, your instructor, classmates, and your mother. All are painting you as a victim." Councilwoman Georgia said with her brows drawn down as if she was thinking.

The room went silent for several minutes. I took the opportunity to study the council members more closely. Georgia was genuine and truly wanting to see an outcome that was just. Borus looked irritated to be there. He didn't seem to care that a member of the pack had been far more aggressive towards another pack member than was warranted, while Jet looked amused and curious.

Borus narrowed his eyes at me as he strummed his fingers against the table. "Did she render you unconscious?" I remained quiet. "Did she punch you, leaving bruises on your face?" Again, I said nothing. These questions weren't to get my side of the story. No one from the council had even asked for my side of the event yet. "Are you just going to stand there and not answer our questions?" Borus roared in frustration.

Cora growled in my head. *"I may not like Marissa, but everyone deserves a fair trial, and this isn't it."*

I took a deep breath. Easton's scent from his blazer filled my lungs, it had a calming effect on my nerves. "Your questions aren't designed to know my truth. They are designed to confirm someone else's." I said, crossing my arms over my chest. "If you want to get this over with quickly, might I suggest you allow me to tell you my side of the story? That way you can get the full picture of what happened."

Jet laughed while Borus glared. "Go ahead, girl. We have a fair idea of what happened, but if you want to share, by all means." Jet sat back in his chair with a smile.

"I don't fight." I started and Jet's smile widened. "I hate it. I made a deal with Alpha Callum and both Gammas so that I wouldn't have to participate in Sparring class. Instead, I meet privately with Gamma Jason for lessons. We had a substitute teacher who was unaware of my alternative schedule. Like a teacher should, he insisted that I spar since I was in the class." I took a deep breath and then continued. "Marissa volunteered to be my partner. The instructor told me to raise my guard, and when I did, he started the match. The moment Marissa made a move towards me, I dropped my guard and allowed her to hit me. I dropped to my knees, giving her the opening to get behind me to choke me out and I let her." I said and silence followed.

"Why would you purposely lower your guard knowing you were in a fight?" Borus asked, looking confused.

"Fighting is not something I like to do." I said looking at Borus. "Part of a fight is knowing your opponent and knowing if the fight is worth fighting. Knowing how to manipulate your opponent into doing exactly what you want them to do. Sparring with Marissa wasn't worth it."

"And you manipulated the fight so that you were beaten up and knocked unconscious?" Jet asked, leaning forward. His gaze was sharp and focused.

"Yes, sir. I did what I did, knowing I would be beaten up and knocked unconscious." I said looking down at the floor.

"Carly, explain to us what you mean." Georgia's soft voice was filled with curiosity as well.

"Marissa was close to her shift. I knew that would make her more aggressive than usual. Her wolf wouldn't like being challenged by the person she sees as weak and unworthy. I dropped my guard but did not submit." Seeing the questions in Georgia's eyes I continued quickly. "Submitting and begging Marissa or my instructor to let me back out, was something I wasn't willing to lower myself to. I stood tall and allowed the blows she dealt before giving her an opening to end the fight in a way that she tends to favor." I finished explaining.

The council was quiet for several minutes as they observed me. "Marissa's level of aggression could have killed you if your instructor hadn't pulled her off of you." Georgia informed me with a raised brow. I hadn't known that Easton had pulled Marissa off me, but I didn't let my surprise show. "Even if you willingly took the blows, that level of aggression cannot go unpunished."

"I am curious, Miss Brooks." Jet spoke up. "Who do you put the blame on in this case?"

"Me, sir." I didn't hesitate. "I entered the match knowing that Marissa was much more aggressive that day. I could have informed my instructor of my agreement with the Alpha and Gammas. I could have refused to fight in the first place."

"Hmm." Jet said. "Well, that is it for me. I do wish for you to be present when we speak with the others." He looked to the other council members and seeing them nod, gestured to the seating behind me. "Have a seat."

I sat in the middle of the second row. As the doors opened and people started to file in, the air conditioner kicked on. Unfortunately, I was sitting under the vent. I pulled the jacket tighter around myself as I stared at the ground. Mom came and sat next to me and put a hand on my back. I looked over at her with a tight smile. My earlier confidence was fading, and anxiety replaced it.

I noticed that Max, Mike, and Easton sat directly in front of us. Alpha Callum and Luna Maria sat a few seats down from them with Gamma Jason and Gamma Holly. Marissa and her parents were sitting on the other side of the room. She sent me a glare before smoothing her features and facing forward.

The council members were speaking quietly to each other for several minutes before Georgia and Jet retook their seats. Borus remained standing as he addressed the room.

"Miss Carly Brooks, as a council, we want you to sit up front in that chair." He pointed to a chair that was off to the side facing the room. From that spot, I would be able to see the audience, the council, and the person they were interviewing, and they would all be able to see me.

I swallowed hard as everyone turned to look at me. My gaze met Easton's. Irritation flashed in his eyes. Maybe he was mad that I was still wearing his jacket. Well, he was just going to have to deal with it because I wasn't going to give it back to him in front of everyone. I slowly stood and walked to the chair but hesitated before taking a seat.

"For someone who took over their interview with the council, you seem awfully shy all of a sudden." Jet said loudly, and my face burned with embarrassment.

Sitting quickly, I kept my face down and resisted the urge to cover my face with my hands. I should have left my hair down so I could have used it to shield my face. Glancing up, I quickly found Easton. He was watching me. When our eyes met, the corner of his lips turned up and he gave me the slightest nod. I was marginally comforted by the small gesture. If he was comforting me, maybe he had been irritated with something else.

"Why do I feel like we are on display?" Cora asked.

"Because we are. The question is why?" I told her as I glared at Jet. He smirked back at me.

Mom was called to the front and asked questions about my character, habits, and schedule. Alpha and the Gammas were also asked questions about me. I shifted uncomfortably in my seat and pulled the jacket tighter around myself, breathing deeply. I prayed the world would open up and swallow me whole, but life wasn't that kind.

So far, I learned that everyone saw me as quiet, introverted, kind and willing to help others when needed. Gamma Jason expanded on my resistance to training. He chuckled when he told them that if I felt threatened, I could defend myself.

My face felt like it was on fire with embarrassment. How did this trial end up about me, instead of Marissa? Every time I looked up, Jet was studying me. I could almost see the gears turning in his head. What was he trying to figure out? I got the impression that we knew each other but that couldn't be. I had never met Jet before.

Next, Marissa was called up. The council asked her about her relationship with me and about her actions that day. Marissa hung her head and kept her voice penitent. "I am sorry for hurting a fellow student." she said quietly.

"If you were able to help decide who was at fault in this case, who would you choose?" Jet asked as he studied her closely.

"I don't like to point fingers, but I do not think I should be held responsible for my sparring partner's inability to protect herself in the most basic of moves." Marissa glared at me before blinking and clearing her expression. "I should have listened to Easton when he told me to stop, but Carly shouldn't have been seeking attention."

"You think that woman, over there, seeks attention?" Jet asked with a laugh in his voice. I sank lower into my chair as I felt everyone's eyes on me. Ducking my head, I pretended to wipe hair off my forehead in order to hide my face more. Why did he have to keep drawing attention to me? "Thank you. You may take your seat." He dismissed her with a wave of his hand. "Easton Shepherd, please come forward."

I watched as Easton stood and walked to the front of the room. He had rolled his shirt sleeves up to his elbows, showing off his toned forearms. His shirt fit him perfectly. He was fit before summer, but now his clothes almost seemed to mold to him. I blinked and pulled my gaze from him. Cora was practically drooling and waxed on about how cute Easton was. I gave my head a little shake and told her to be quiet so that I could listen to the rest of the trial.

"You were the instructor the day of the incident?" Georgia asked.

"Yes, ma'am." He was confident and looked at each council member as he answered their questions.

They asked him a lot of the same things they had asked everyone else. They also asked about his relationship with both me and Marissa. He said he didn't have a relationship with Marissa, and he was barely above enemy status with me, which made everyone but me, Max, and Mike laugh. Only the four of us knew how true that statement was.

Jet eyed Easton up and down before sitting forward. "Just like I asked earlier, who would you say is at fault here?"

"I am." Easton said firmly. "As the instructor, it was my job to keep everyone in my care safe and I failed. I should not have pushed Miss Brooks into sparring when she had told me she didn't want to. I should have seen the signs of Miss Hampton's upcoming shift and had her sit out, so she wouldn't hurt anyone. The fault of Miss Brooks's injuries lies solely with me." I was watching Easton carefully. Did he really feel responsible for what had happened?

"You are still quite young. I am glad you are willing to take responsibility for your actions. That is a mark of a good leader." Georgia commented as she sat back. After a minute of silence, she continued. "Do you think that Marissa Hampton should be sent to the Garrison Pack for two months?" Georgia asked.

I blinked in surprise. The Garrison Pack was more of a work camp where prisoners were sent for punishment. Marissa didn't deserve that. Sure, she was a bully and needed to be taken down a notch, but two months at the Garrison Pack was extreme.

Easton glanced in my direction quickly and his jaw tightened. He remained quiet for several minutes. He looked like he was waging an internal battle. His hands balled into fists. "No, ma'am." he finally said through a clenched jaw.

Jet looked between me and Easton several times. "What would you recommend then?" He asked Easton.

Easton flexed his hand before balling it back into a fist. "Taking into account that Miss Hampton was near her shift, and that Miss Brooks willingly let down her guard, I feel like a more suitable punishment should be found." Easton's whole body radiated tension.

Jet's eyes filled with understanding as he smiled and shook his head. Jet may have understood, but I sure didn't. I thought Easton wanted Marissa to pay for what she did. His actions in the gym a few weeks ago sure hinted at that.

Borus stood and dismissed the meeting. We were to meet back here in the morning for the verdict. I remained in my seat as I observed the crowd. Jet quickly moved around the table and approached Easton and Max. Jet glanced in my direction before saying something to Easton, who gave a small nod. The councilman laughed and clapped Easton on the shoulder before approaching me.

"Do you agree with your instructor's suggestion about Miss Hampton?" Jet asked me. I stood from my chair, not liking the feeling of him looking down at me.

This man's closeness put me on edge. He watched me too closely and I hated the attention he had drawn to me. "Was this really necessary?" I snapped at him before I could stop myself. I shook my head and tried to move around him, but he blocked my path. "Let me pass, sir." I growled out.

"Now, now, Miss Brooks." He tsked. "You are drawing attention to us." He smirked.

I glanced around and noticed that Max, Mike, Alpha Callum, and my mom were watching while Easton glared at us. My face turned red, and I ducked my head. *"Cora, help me."* I begged her as I felt tears sting my eyes again. I was so emotionally done at the moment.

Cora growled as she paced in my head. *"If you weren't in a skirt I would suggest climbing over the chairs. I do not like this guy. His aura is stronger than anyone I have ever known. I don't like it."* She continued to growl. *"Move the chairs out of the way and put distance between him and us."*

I moved to my left and slid between the chairs in the first row. I walked down the aisle to the center of the room and headed for the door. A powerful aura pushed on me, but I wasn't in the mood to play a submissive Omega, so I kept going. I ignored Jet telling me to stop as I shoved open the door.

As soon as I was in the hallway, I slipped my shoes off and moved quickly outside. I heard mom's and Gamma Holly's voices calling after me before the front door closed. I needed to get away to have a few moments of privacy to collect myself.

Without thinking, I followed the path to the waterfall as quickly as I could in my pencil skirt. Once there, I threw my shoes to the ground and stepped into the shallow end of the pool. The icy cold water caused me to suck in a quick breath. The shock of the water helped calm my frustration and embarrassment.

What was Jet's deal? He purposely kept putting me on the spot and drawing attention to me. My anger began to build again. I let out a frustrated growl as I took a couple steps forward, the water rising to mid-thigh. I didn't care that my skirt was getting wet. The only thing that stopped me from diving completely under the waterfall was the fact that I was wearing Easton's expensive blazer and the blouse my mom had just bought. She would kill me if I ruined it.

"For someone who is usually cold, I find it odd that you are willingly stepping into that freezing water." Max's voice said from behind me.

I let out a little laugh as I felt my first tear slip onto my cheek. "The shock helps center me." I said without turning around.

"Easton isn't here." Cora pouted.

"If you say so." He commented skeptically. "Wanna talk about it?"

"Talk about what?" I asked as I wiped my cheek and took a slow deep breath. "Why some crazy councilman seemed to be way too interested in making me uncomfortable? Or why he insisted on putting me on display? Or why he boxed me in after the meeting?"

Max stayed quiet for a few minutes. He hissed as water splashed behind me. I glanced over at him to see that he had rolled up his pant legs and was walking out to where I stood. He stopped before the water touched his slacks at his knees.

"Next time he can come check on you himself." He grumbled under his breath, but I still heard him. "You are insane you know that?" He told me with a smile. "Just so you know, Jet isn't a real councilman. He is visiting from the Royal Pack and stood in for Councilman Patrick because Patrick was out on pack business."

My brows knit in confusion. I reached down and ran my fingers through the water. "I don't understand why he is even interested in me." I said quietly.

"He talked with your mom after you left. She looked upset before she too, disappeared." Max shrugged. "I have met Jet a few times, but I have never seen him act the way he did today. He is usually distant and quiet, watching everything and everyone, but not really talkative."

"Was it just me or did he put me on display by calling me up to sit in front of everyone?" I asked, turning to face Max.

"He did seem to be making some sort of statement, but I'm not sure what it was. Even dad was confused as to why you were having to sit up front. Why didn't you stop when he pushed out his aura? Dad even submitted to him."

A movement just over Max's left shoulder caught my eye. I focused my attention on where I had seen it, but couldn't make out anything out of the ordinary. "Max." I said so softly I was sure that the waterfall drowned out my voice. I was immediately tense again. Something didn't feel right.

Max's posture stiffened and his eyes shifted to a darker brown. He stood still for a moment before his eyes focused on me again. "If you are done with your soak, I think we should head back." I nodded and he grabbed my arm as we made our way back to shore.

He shoved his feet in his shoes and grabbed my heels in one hand and my hand in the other. He guided me down the path quickly while scanning the trees. He handed me my shoes when we made it back to my house. "Stay away from the waterfall for now." he said firmly. I gave him a nod and went inside.

I wasn't sure what Max had sensed at the falls. But I was glad I hadn't been alone. I had a feeling that danger had been close. It felt like we were being watched. Even Cora felt uneasy.

Chapter 5

Morning came and the rain from the night before continued. I felt chilled all the way to my bones and my muscles ached. I took a quick shower before I got dressed in my normal shirt and jeans. As I left my bathroom, I caught sight of Easton's blazer draped over the back of my desk chair. I couldn't help but smile as Cora sighed and waxed on about how thoughtful Easton had been when he gave us use of the jacket.

I pulled on one of my hoodies instead of my father's and went downstairs for breakfast. Mom was cooking at the stove when I walked into the kitchen.

"Morning, sweetheart." She said with a forced smile.

"Morning." I said slowly as I narrowed my eyes at her. Had she been crying? "Is everything okay?"

Mom loaded a plate with eggs and bacon before bringing it to me. "It will be once all this business with Marissa is over." She said, turning her back to me.

I ate quickly and pulled on a pair of boots. Mom protested that I wasn't going to dress up again. I made the case that it was raining, and it would be better to avoid getting my nicer clothes all wet. She agreed only because we were out of time.

I was mostly soaked by the time we got there. I was shivering as I slid onto a chair at the back of the room. Mom looked worriedly at me but didn't say anything. The air conditioner kicked on and I scowled at the floor. Dang all these normal wolves and their higher body temperature.

Marissa was called to the front. She was told that her unchecked aggression was what was being punished. She would not be in any of my classes for the rest of the school year and she would have to work at the packhouse as a servant for three months. I let out a sigh of relief when the meeting concluded.

Easton turned to talk to Max and our eyes met. He scowled before he whispered to Max and Mike. Max turned quickly to look at me and his brows rose. I looked away and hugged myself tighter. *"I need to get home and get warm before I end up sick."* I told Cora.

"You are sick." Cora corrected. *"Stressing makes you sick and the cold weather probably isn't helping."*

"Hey mom, I'm going to head home and get in some dry clothes." I whispered to her.

"When you are done, heat up the soup in the fridge. It will help." Mom nodded to the door, and I stood, not needing to be told twice.

I took a deep breath before racing out into the storm. I did not stop running until I made it to my porch. I tried the handle and let out a sigh as the handle turned. I made sure to lock the door behind me before climbing the stairs to my room. First off, a hot shower, then warm clothes. I glanced in the mirror as I turned on the shower. I was drenched, my lips were slightly blue, and I was shivering. I looked like a half-drowned cat.

The warm water burned my cold skin as I stood in the spray. I stayed there until the water turned cold. I changed into a long sleeve shirt and sweatpants before pulling on another sweatshirt. I blow dried my hair and pulled a beanie on.

As I was walking down the stairs to heat up the soup, the front door opened. Mom walked in followed by Max, Easton, and Gamma Jason. I stopped on the last step and eyed everyone.

"Oh good, you're done." Mom said with a smile as she showed our guests to the living room.

"Yeah, I was just about to heat up the soup you said to eat." I commented, eyeing the men warily. I was still shivering a little and all I wanted to do was curl up under a blanket and sleep. "I'm sorry. Did I miss something after the meeting or…?" I entered the kitchen and walked over to the fridge. I pulled it open, looking for the soup.

"No, Gamma Jason asked why you left so quickly." Mom moved to my side and lowered her voice so I was the only one who could hear. "Your lips were blue, and they noticed." She eyed me with a practiced eye. "Carr, you are still too pale, but at least you look mostly back to normal." She reached around me and grabbed a container. "I'll get this heated up for you. You talk with our guests."

I sighed and moved back to the living room. My favorite chair was available, and I settled myself into it before looking at the occupants of the room. All eyes were on me, and I fidgeted.

"You didn't need to come all this way in the rain, Gamma Jason. You could have sent me a text." I said with a small smile. I avoided looking over at Easton and Max.

"I did text you." Gamma Jason said with worry in his voice. "I have never seen anyone look more like a popsicle."

I shivered again and unconsciously pulled my blanket out of the basket next to my chair. I draped it over my legs as I tried to come up with something to say. Mom walked in and saved me from having to comment. She handed me a bowl of steaming soup before sitting in a chair close to mine. She was worried. I could tell by the deep lines around her mouth.

"It was nice of you to check in on Carr, Gamma Jason." Mom said with a smile. "And you too boys. It is comforting to know that she has people looking out for her."

I rolled my eyes at my mom. "Thank you, Gamma. But I assure you that at this moment in time, I am perfectly fine." I tried to reassure both mom and Gamma Jason.

"I don't think I have seen a werewolf wear so many layers before." Max commented, and I sent him a glare.

"Are we still on for training this afternoon, Gamma?" I asked, turning my attention back to Jason.

He eyed me carefully for a moment. "If you are up for it." He stated with uncertainty.

"I will meet you at the normal time then." I said as I got to my feet. Mom made a tsking sound. "I'm going to eat this in the kitchen. Thanks again for stopping by."

I set my bowl on the table and wrapped my arms around myself. "You are not fine." Easton said quietly from behind me.

I spun around to face him. I had not expected anyone to follow me. We eyed each other for a minute before Easton stepped close to me. I could feel his heat before he wrapped his arms around me. I stiffened at the unexpected contact.

Another shiver shook me, and he tightened his hold. After a minute I relaxed against him, soaking in his warmth. Yeah, a personal heater was nice.

Cora even sighed in relief. It was amazing that she could feel the same level of cold I felt, even though I hadn't shifted yet.

"Thank you." I whispered as I rested my head against his chest.

"How are you so cold?" Easton asked quietly and I shrugged in response. He pulled me tighter against him and I sighed. He rubbed one of his hands up and down my arm in an effort to help warm me. "You seriously looked like a popsicle at the meeting."

"Thanks." I said dryly, causing him to chuckle. Voices from the other room caused us both to stiffen.

Easton released me and took a step back. I immediately felt cold again. "I should probably go; I told them I went to the bathroom." He glanced back at the kitchen door quickly.

"I can't believe you lied to your dad." I whispered with a laugh. Easton smiled at me before walking to the door. He paused and looked back at me, winked, and then disappeared.

"That was so nice." Cora purred.

"What has gotten into you, Cora? You used to hate Easton." I said as I sat at the table.

"I don't know. He seems so different since he has been back. Less like an annoying teenager desperate for attention and more mature."

"I have noticed that too. Mike and Max are as well. They all seem more sensitive to the needs of the pack." I took a sip of the soup.

"I like Easton, I like him a lot." Cora laughed. *"I really like how protective and warm he is."*

"Down girl." I laughed. "We aren't even eighteen yet. We have always said we wouldn't get involved with anyone unless they are our mate." I reminded her and she settled down.

I sat at the table, sipping my soup, until I heard the men leave. Mom came in and looked me over again. She tried to convince me to take it easy, but I needed to get all my training classes in if I wanted to graduate on time.

I went upstairs with the promise to rest until it was time to meet with Gamma Jason, so mom would let me be. Lucky for me, mom had to go to work within the hour and the house became blessedly quiet when she left. I set an alarm and fell asleep.

My alarm went off and I pulled my hair into a ponytail. I put my boots on at the front door and shoved my tennis shoes into a bag. Thankfully, the rain had stopped for the time being.

Taking advantage of the break in the storm, I sprinted down the path towards the packhouse. I punched in the code to the side door just as the rain started again. I wrapped my arms around myself as I walked down the hall. I slipped into the sparring gym and froze.

"And I told you that today is not the day for this!" Gamma Jason yelled.

"Jason, calm down." Alpha Callum was trying to defuse whatever tense situation I just walked into.

"Just because he is from the Royal Pack does not mean he can come into my private lesson and demand to 'have a whack' at it." Jason snapped.

I blinked in surprise. I had never seen Jason so angry before. I debated whether I should leave or make myself known, but a third voice made my decision for me. "Well, if it isn't the girl herself." Jet chuckled. "Come over here, Carly."

I set my bag down and took off my muddy boots. I couldn't hear what they were whispering, but I could still tell Jason was mad. Just having Jet here caused my hackles to rise, combining that with messing with Jason, and I was ready for a good run to let off steam. Jason was a good man and Jet messing with him was not okay. I pushed past my fatigue and walked over to the three men.

"I said no." Jason growled.

"Why don't we ask Carly?" Jet crossed his arms over his chest and looked at me. I narrowed my eyes at him in return.

"Alpha, do something." Jason demanded. "He is a royal and she is seventeen years old. She isn't even old enough to have her wolf."

"I don't understand." I said looking between the three men.

Alpha Callum turned fully to face me. The expression on his face told me that this was serious. "Jet is the youngest son of the Alpha King. He has asked if he could spar with you today during your training." I glanced over at Jet. "You need to understand that as a royal and an adult werewolf, he will be a lot faster and stronger than you."

I took my time to study Jet. He seemed eager for the fight. *"What do you think, Cora?"* I asked.

"I think this is a test. I think he is trying to figure out if we were able to manipulate the fight with Marissa." Cora responded.

"If I do this, what do I get?" I asked, turning back to Alpha.

"You won't have to train anymore until after graduation." He said without hesitating.

He knew what I would want, and he offered it up.

"I know you aren't feeling well, but let's do it, Carr. The worst that could happen is that we get a little banged up. It's not the first time it has happened." Cora said. *"That and if we refuse, I bet he will hang around until he gets what he wants."*

I could tell she was not a big fan of Jet either. There was something about him that made me want to submit to him, and Cora didn't like it. Even though I didn't like to fight, I still didn't like to submit to others. It was probably his royal blood that gave him that level of power.

I nodded slowly. "Okay." I said watching the smug look on Jet's face. "But I need to warm up first."

Gamma Jason fell into step beside me as I began a slow jog around the gym. "You don't have to do this, Carr." He was practically begging. "You could get seriously injured."

I continued jogging the perimeter. "I will be okay, Gamma." I gave him my most confident smile, even though I was second guessing Cora. We jogged seven laps in silence. "I do not have to win, just participate. At this point, if he doesn't get this chance, he will hang around longer and I rather see him gone." Gamma Jason chuckled. He pulled me to a stop and gave me a hug.

I returned his embrace and moved to the mats. Jet eagerly stepped up and raised his guard. I sat down and began to stretch. Jet's expression went from smug to frustrated. I watched him carefully as I went through my stretches as slowly as I could without making it obvious I was intentionally delaying the match.

He was like most males; he just wanted a fight. I masked my amusement as I watched him begin pacing like a caged animal. Once or twice when he thought I was getting up to start, only for me to go into a different stretch, he growled in frustration.

I straightened up and walked back to my bag. I noticed that Alpha Callum and Gamma Jason were standing off to the side with Beta Harry, Mike, Max, and Easton.

I ignored them as I took off my sweatshirt. I realized I had forgotten to change into my workout clothes before I left home. Feeling uncomfortable with all the males present, I hesitated.

I shook my head, most of the girls at school wore less clothes than I was going to be in. My nicer shirt wasn't something to spar in. Taking a deep breath, I pulled my shirt off, but kept my sweats on. Goosebumps broke out along my skin. I was only in baggy sweatpants and a sports bra, and I was freezing.

"Are we going to do this, or not?" Jet snapped.

"I don't want to pull a muscle." I called back to him with a smirk.

Gamma Jason walked with me to the center of the mat and gave me a pleading look. I looked at Jet, raised my guard, and widened my stance. I was as ready for this as I could be.

Mom and Jason had taught me well, and I could hold my own. I contemplated doing as I had with Marissa but decided against it. I had the feeling he wanted me to do that. Cora wanted to win this fight. He thought I was weak, especially when he saw me cold this morning. Jason gave me one last look before stepping back.

"Fight." Jason called.

Jet advanced quickly and I countered, watching the way he moved. As he lunged for me, I dove between his legs and ended up behind him. I kicked the back of his knees hard, and he fell to the mat. Jet growled in frustration as we both got back to our feet. My heart began to race as my adrenaline kicked in. We circled each other a few times before Jet took a swing at me. Even though I blocked the blow, it still hurt.

"He's not pulling his punches." Cora yelled angrily.

"I realize that." I panted out.

"We need to end this fast, or he will hurt us." Cora warned.

I dodged his attacks as I strategized. If I could get him to the ground, I might be able to get him to tap out. I jumped over his attempt to sweep my feet out from under me and kicked him hard in the chest causing him to stumble back a few steps. If he was going full throttle so could I.

I dropped my guard and stood up straight. "Had enough yet?" I asked with my arms out wide.

Jet took the bait and tackled me. I hit the mat so hard that the wind was knocked out of me. I gasped for air as he climbed on top of me. He grabbed my wrists and yanked hard, pinning my hands above my head. I bit my cheek to keep from crying out as pain shot up my arm. I heard someone yell, but my focus was on Jet.

He had a smug look on his face as he smirked down at me. I noticed that his eyes were darker than normal. No wonder he was punching so hard, his wolf was pushing forward. I smirked back just as I drove my knee up, hitting his rear end.

Jet yelled as he sat back on my hips, releasing my wrist. I bucked my hips throwing him off balance. I trapped his arm and pushed my hips up at the same time, causing us to roll. My arm was hurting so bad and was nearly useless.

"End this, Carly!" Cora yelled.

I wrapped my good arm around Jet's neck. With my other arm I tried to get control of his arm but couldn't. I lifted his head to get a deeper hold. Jet managed to roll us again and I lost my progress. I wrapped my legs around his waist, keeping him close. He delivered several hard blows to my ribs before he reached down to try to free himself from my legs. I quickly threw my leg over his neck as I grabbed the arm that was still up by my head. I hooked my other leg over my foot and squeezed. Seconds later, Jet went limp.

I released him and shoved at his unconscious body. Someone grabbed me under my arms and helped pull me out from under Jet. When I was free, I collapsed back on the mats, breathing hard. I put a hand over my face and started to cry. I hated fighting. I hated to hurt people.

"Carr, where are you hurt?" Jason asked anxiously as I felt hands pulling at mine. I uncovered my face and looked at him. "Where are you hurt?" He asked again.

"Is he, okay?" I asked as I began to shake, which didn't help the pain my battered body was feeling.

"That man just beat you up and you are worried if he is okay?" Jason shook his head.

"I'm sorry." I whispered as I sat up. I groaned and grabbed my side. "I'm so sorry, Jason."

"What do you have to be sorry about, Carr?" he asked, confused.

"I shouldn't have fought him. I should have refused." I wiped the tears off my cheeks. That's when I noticed everyone else had joined us on the mats. Easton looked livid. "I am so sorry. This is all my fault. I shouldn't have, but I hate bullies and he was bullying you." I told Jason.

Jason looked at me incredulously. "You fought a royal because you thought he was bullying me?" I nodded and glanced over at Jet.

He was starting to wake up and Easton moved in between me and Jet. I watched as he regained consciousness slowly. He looked at me in disbelief. "How did you...?" he asked, shock all over his face.

Tears blurred my vision again. "I am so sorry. I shouldn't have." I buried my face in my good hand again as I held my injured arm close to my body.

"Boys, take Carly to the hospital while we have a talk with Jet." Alpha Callum said firmly.

Someone grabbed my hands to help me to my feet and I cried out in pain. My side was killing me, and I was certain my elbow had been dislocated when Jet had pulled on my wrists. They let go of me and everyone gathered around with worried expressions. Even Jet looked concerned. I took several deep breaths before getting to my feet. Easton reached out to steady me and I looked up at him.

"Someone, please pop my elbow back?" I said as I glanced around the group. "And I want my hoodie." Max ran off. Alpha came to my side and lifted my arm carefully with a tight expression. I gritted my teeth against the pain. "Just do it, Alpha." I said quietly and I squeezed my eyes shut, preparing for the pain I knew was coming.

Jason grabbed my hand, giving gentle but firm traction. I whimpered softly. Alpha Callum slowly began pressing on the elbow and my breathing increased. I heard and felt it pop back into place and I let out a cry before my legs gave out. Strong arms wrapped around me, and I looked up to see Easton. I leaned heavily against him, allowing him to support me as I cradled my injured arm close to my chest.

Max returned and handed my hoodie to Easton. Carefully, they managed to slip it over my head. I vaguely heard Alpha tell someone to take me home. My legs were swept out from under me, but I didn't fall. Instead, I was lifted into someone's arms and a whimper escaped my lips.

"It's okay, Carr. I got you." Easton whispered in my ear. Just the sound of his voice eased my anxiety. I closed my eyes and allowed him to carry me.

A jolt of pain shot up my side and I gasped as my eyes flew open. Easton was there. His arms were still partially around me. "Holy crap, that hurt." I groaned.

"I was just putting you down on the couch." Easton said with an apology heavy in his voice.

"Just do it then." I said as I squeezed my eyes shut. He finished sitting me down and I breathed through the pain. Once the pain passed, I looked back up to see Mike and Max next to Easton. All three of them were watching me with concern. I gave them a smile. *"Other than the dislocated elbow, how bad is it, Cora?"* I asked.

"No broken bones or internal bleeding. But there will be bruising." She informed me. *"That Jet guy can sure pack a punch."*

"Max, can you go grab the first aid kit for me?" He gave me a nod before walking out of the front room. "Mike, Easton, help me take my hoodie off." They exchanged looks but helped me sit up and we got the hoodie off by the time Max put the kit on the coffee table. "Good. Now, there is a dark green jar with a black lid."

"This?" Max held up the bottle and I nodded.

"I need help putting it on my bruises and there should be a red bottle. The red bottle needs to go on my elbow." I took a deep breath and slowly let it out. I was really starting to feel like crap.

Max handed the green jar to Easton who unscrewed the lid and took a sniff. He coughed and wrinkled his nose. "What is this stuff?" he asked in disgust.

"That is something that will reduce the bruising." I said with a small smile. "Here." I reached my hand in the jar and scooped out a large amount of the cream. I started to try to spread it over my ribs and side where the discoloration was already making an appearance. Seeing me struggling, Easton grabbed my wrist, scraped the cream off my fingers, and began rubbing it in. I winced. My side was incredibly tender. "There should also be a bottle of ibuprofen in there, too."

"What are all these jars?" Max asked.

"Witch's potions." Mike said, eyeing them with misgiving.

Max and Easton paused what they were doing and looked over at him before looking at me. Easton continued rubbing the cream into my side.

"Here's the thing." I winced again as Easton put too much pressure on a particularly tender spot. He mouthed sorry. "There are good witches and bad witches just like there are good and bad werewolves." My eyes met Easton's. "The witch that gave us these medicines saved my life more than once before we got to this pack."

I reached forward and twisted the lid back on the jar in Easton's hand before taking the red one from Max. I grabbed a glove out of the first aid box. "What are you doing?" Easton asked.

"This one burns. It's best if it doesn't touch skin that it doesn't need to." He gave me a hard look. "With this, my elbow should be back to normal by tomorrow." Easton took the glove from me and put it on. "All magic has a price. The price of using this for accelerated healing is pain."

He carefully opened the jar and scooped out a small amount. I took several quick breaths as I watched his hand move closer to my elbow. I remembered the painful sensation this cream caused. I had to use it last year after my encounter with Marissa in the locker room. She had cornered me after class and Gamma Holly had found me unconscious on the floor a while later. I had to use the cream on my knee because it was so painful and swollen that I could hardly walk.

Easton saw my anxiety and hesitated. I gave him a nod and his jaw clenched. "Are you s…" He asked.

"Just do it, Easton." I snapped and then hissed as he touched his hand to my elbow. The burning was instant and intense. He moved quickly, spreading fire everywhere he touched.

Max moved in front of me and grabbed my face. "Breathe, nice and slow, Carly." he said calmly. "Slow breath in, slow breath out." I tried to follow his coaching, but I couldn't draw in a breath. Spots started to appear in my vision, and I squeezed my eyes closed as I fought to remain conscious. "Did I tell you guys about how crazy Carly is?" Max asked.

"Dude she just took out a royal, I think we saw how crazy this chick is." Mike said dryly.

"I wasn't referring to that insanity." Max said. "She likes to walk into the nearly frozen waterfall pond to clear her mind." I let out a laugh as I felt tears on my cheeks. I had no idea when I started to cry. "I even told her that it was strange for a girl who gets cold to enjoy polar bear swimming."

"I wasn't polar bear swimming." I whispered. The burning was starting to fade. I opened my eyes and sank back against the couch with a tired sigh. "Thigh deep is not even swimming."

"I bet if you didn't have on Easton's blazer you would have been." Max smiled.

I reached for my hoodie and Easton helped me put it on. "I was wondering what happened to that jacket." Easton sat beside me on the couch.

"If you really want it, it's up in my room." I said as I closed my eyes. "And you are wrong, Max. If I wasn't in clothes my mom would have killed me if I ruined, I would have sat behind the falls."

"You got your skirt all wet." Max pointed out causing the guys to laugh.

A knock on the door had everyone sobering. "What now?" I groaned.

"We got you, Carly." Max said. "Mike, clear this first-aid kit while I answer the door."

I heard Mike cleaning up the kit as Max walked out of the room. I turned to look at Easton who was watching me. "Thank you." I said before laying my head on his shoulder and closing my eyes.

"Just promise me you won't do that again." Easton said softly. "I don't think I can handle watching you get beat up again."

"How is she doing? Has the pack doctor been by yet?" Gamma Jason's voice reached me from the front door. I opened my eyes in time to see Alpha Callum, Jason, and Jet walk into my living room. I felt Easton tense beside me when Jet entered. When they saw me sitting up, Jason moved directly to me. He grabbed me by my face and pressed a kiss to my forehead. "You gave me a heart attack."

I went to put my arms around his neck to give him a hug, but gasped and dropped my injured left arm. I still gave him a one-armed hug before sitting back again. "I said I was sorry. I know I should have followed your advice and not allowed Jet to goad me."

"How are you feeling?" Alpha Callum asked from his position by Jet.

"A bit sore, but overall, pretty good." I gave him a smile.

"Yeah, as long as you don't move." Cora scoffed.

"We would like to know what happened." Alpha Callum said gently.

I looked around the room. "You were all there. I'm sure you all saw what happened."

"How did you overpower me?" Jet cut me off.

"I didn't." I looked at him. "There is no way I could ever overpower you or anyone in this room. Like I told you yesterday, you have to know your opponent if you want any chance of defeating them."

"You don't know me." Jet said as he crossed his arms over his chest.

I glared at him. "I have been reading you from the moment I met you." I told him. "You were curious after hearing Gamma Jason's report on my progress in training and why I would allow a peer to best me. I fueled your curiosity when I explained I had manipulated the fight with Marissa to end how I wanted it to. You wanted to know what would happen if I was faced with someone of superior strength and power." I raised my brow. "Am I right?"

"It doesn't take a rocket scientist to know that I was intrigued with your story." He glanced at Alpha.

"True. You were also trying to bully Gamma Jason into a match with me. That was your first mistake. I do not like bullies." I tried to shift positions, but pain shot threw my side and stole my breath for a moment. "I deliberately took my time warming up and stretching to test your patience. You were like a caged animal ready to be freed. Just like most males, you allowed your lust for a fight to cloud your judgment. Your wolf lost patience and took over a bit. The moment I realized you were putting your full strength into each attack; I knew I needed to get you to the ground and end the fight. If I didn't, I would get hurt. You are far stronger than I am."

"That's why you dropped your fighting posture." Jason said in amazement. "You gave him an opening he wouldn't be able to resist."

"Exactly. Most people think that the ground is a dangerous place during a fight, when in fact it is one of the best. The hold I used is one of my favorites because it allows those who are not as strong to use leverage to their advantage. All I had to do was hold on and wait for you to go limp." I said with a smirk.

The room was quiet for several moments before the door burst open and my mom came running into the room with eyes blazing.

Chapter 6

I jumped to my feet and moved to stand between mom and Jet. She was out for blood, and she had zoned in on her target. She stopped just before colliding with me. I grabbed my side as I doubled over, groaning.

"What happened?" Mom snapped, turning her glare on Alpha and Gamma.

"Mom, calm down. Nothing but a little sparring practice." I said as I slowly straightened.

"I get a call at work to tell me that my daughter fought a royal representative that is visiting for the week." She turned to me. "Did you break anything?" She turned worried eyes on me.

I shook my head. "A dislocated elbow and some bruising." She pulled me into a gentle hug. "I'm fine, Mom. I put the creams on already. Calm down, I am fine."

She released me and pushed me behind her as she stepped up to Jet and punched him in the face. Everyone watched in shocked silence. Jet wiped the blood off his split lip as he straightened back up.

"How dare you challenge an underaged wolf to a fight? Someone of your station should know better. For crying out loud, she doesn't even have her wolf yet. Do you realize how long it will take her to heal from her injuries? She is not Broo...Get out of my house!" Mom yelled.

"You are right, Mrs. Brooks. I was careless and could have seriously injured *your* daughter." Jet said. "I'm sorry, Carly, for hurting you." He looked at me and there was something in his eyes that told me this wasn't the last time I would see him. He gave my mother a nod before walking out the door.

"Mom, that was unnecessary." I said quietly as I touched her arm gently.

"I thought it was well deserved." Easton said from where he stood by the couch.

"Violence is not always the answer. I had already beaten him, even though I should never have engaged in the fight in the first place." I glared at Easton, and he shrugged.

"You beat him?" Mom turned her full attention back to me.

"I let him take me to the ground and used a triangle choke." I said with a small smile.

Mom laughed as she hugged me again. "That's my girl."

"I was wondering where that move came from, because I haven't taught it to her." Jason said. "In fact, there are several moves I am curious to know where she picked up."

Mom let me go with a sigh. "Carly, has been training since she was three." Mom said. "Alpha, Gamma, I think it is time we talked."

"As fun as that sounds, I am going to bed." I said as I turned and headed for the stairs while cradling my left arm. No one stopped me, and I made it up to my room with no issues. I was digging in my drawer for a pajama shirt when a knock sounded on my door jam. I glanced over to see Easton and Max standing there. "Your jacket is over there." I pointed to the chair as I pulled a long-sleeved shirt out of the drawer.

They entered my room and Easton picked up his jacket. "Thanks, but that wasn't why we came up here." I gave him a questioning look. He transferred his weight from one foot to the other uncomfortably for a second before continuing. "Your mom and our dads went to the packhouse to have a private word. Your mom insisted that you not be left alone. She said something about you nearly freezing this morning and then the fight and being worried you might become sick." He rubbed his neck, avoiding my gaze.

"Thank you, mom." I grumbled to Cora. *"So overprotective."*

"Thank you, mom." Cora laughed. *"I don't mind Easton staying."*

I walked towards the bathroom. "Fine. I'll be out in a minute." I closed and locked the bathroom door. I changed into my zero-degree spandex shirt and a pair of sweatpants. I took a few minutes to look at my bruises and sighed. Jet really did a number on me.

I opened the door and walked across the room to the nightstand. I grabbed the remote and tossed it to Max, who caught it. "Just keep the volume down to a reasonable level."

"What, no hoodie to bed?" Easton sent me a teasing smile and I stuck my tongue out at him which only caused his smile to grow.

I climbed into bed slowly and groaned as I lay down. Pain spasmed up my whole left side for several minutes. I could not wait for the creams to kick in. When I glanced over at the guys, they were watching me with concern. "Stop staring at me like that." I glared at them. "Turn the TV on and let me sleep." I closed my eyes, and I heard the TV click on. I heard them changing the channels, but I didn't hear when they finally settled on something.

I blinked a few times as I woke up. I stretched and rolled over. My side twinged slightly, but most of the pain was gone. I stifled a scream when I saw Easton sitting in my computer chair next to my bed. His grin was nearly ear to ear as he watched me.

My heart tripped over itself when I saw Max and Mike in my room as well. I covered my face with my blankets and cursed my mom over and over again.

"We could wake up to a worse sight than Easton.*"* Cora pointed out.

"Thanks Cora, that is so helpful right now." I said sarcastically, and she laughed.

"You have to admit that with that dimpled smile of his, he is gorgeous." Cora continued.

"You are ridiculous. I hope we find our mate soon after we turn eighteen so you can stop wanting to cuddle up to every guy around." I told her.

"You make sounds in your sleep." Mike said with a laugh in his voice.

Great, the future Alpha, Beta, and Gamma have witnessed some of my embarrassing tendencies. "Kill me now." I groaned.

"Come on guys, leave her alone." Easton said.

"What, you are defending her now?" Mike asked, still laughing.

Max piped up even though he too was laughing. "You saw what she did to a royal, right? Maybe she will unleash that awesomeness on you."

"Only if you mess with my dad." Easton shot back, and all the guys burst out laughing.

I threw the covers off and stood, glaring at them. "Just because your dad likes me more than he likes you doesn't mean you have to be jealous." I shot at Easton.

Easton's eyes narrowed as he looked at me. "There is no way he likes you more. He didn't even know who you were before summer hit."

I laughed as I moved to my closet. I grabbed my underwear and workout clothes before shoving them in a bag. I didn't want the guys to see anything. I walked to my bathroom, but before I closed the door, I turned back to the guys. "Oh, he likes me way more." I closed the door and got changed into my running clothes before pulling back on my sweatpants, shirt, and hoodie. When I exited, all three guys were eyeing me. "What?"

"You seem to be doing better." Max said in surprise.

"The bruising is bad, but the creams take most of the sting away." I shrugged. "Thanks for helping me with them." I said as I moved to my door and left my room.

"Where are you going?" Mike yelled after me. "Your mom said for you to rest."

I needed a run, and I preferred running at the gym. The stress of the fight and trial had me wound up, even though I wasn't feeling the greatest. I picked up my gym shoes, put them in my bag, and zipped it closed. The guys were halfway down the stairs when I gave them a salute and walked out the door.

I ran barefoot down the path as I headed for the packhouse. I could hear them calling after me, but I didn't stop. When I got to the packhouse I glanced behind me but didn't see anyone. I punched in the code and entered quickly. The guys would be here soon, and chances were they weren't going to be happy with me, but I needed this.

I took off my outer layers and put on my shoes. I climbed onto my favorite treadmill, the one that faced out the window with a view of the forest. I put my earbuds in and started my running playlist. I had been running for a good twenty minutes before a hand reached over and hit the stop button. I groaned as I slowed to a walk and then a stop. I pulled my earbud from my ear and turned to face Gamma Jason.

"I got a text from Easton saying you took off and that they couldn't find you. Your scent was impossible to track." He folded his arms over his chest. "It's a good thing I knew where to look."

"I am sorry I caused them to worry, but I honestly thought they were right behind me. I needed a good run. The past several days has been stressful." I looked longingly at the machine.

Gamma Jason sighed and pinched the bridge of his nose. "You really are something, you know that?" He shook his head and lowered his hand. "Your mother said you would be okay, that you had some sort of cream to aid in your healing. I want you to be honest with me. How are you doing?"

"Just sore, I promise. The bruising looks much worse than it feels." I said honestly. I lifted my shirt a little to show him as the door opened and Easton entered, followed by Mike and Max. All three looked thunderous. I stepped off the treadmill and moved slightly behind Jason. They stomped across the room and stopped several feet from us.

"Glad you got my message. For future reference, if Carr is feeling overwhelmed or stressed, she likes to run, and you can usually find her here." Jason motioned around the gym.

"You are just going to tell us that we should have known she would come here and not reprimand her for disappearing on us?" Easton fumed. "If I had done that, you would have grounded me for at least a week or two."

"Carr said she was sorry, and she said she thought you were right behind her." Jason said as he put an arm around my shoulders, and I leaned into his side.

I smiled. "Does that mean I can continue to run?" I looked up at him with hopeful eyes.

He sighed and nodded his head slowly. "Sure, sweetheart."

"Thank you, Jason." I said as I hopped up on the treadmill.

"I don't believe this; you really do like her more than you like us." Max said in disbelief.

Jason gave me a wink. "It's not about liking Carr more. She is just the daughter I always wished I had. You three are like sons to me, but there is something about a daughter that pulls at a man's heart strings." I blew Jason a kiss before starting the machine again, but Jason pressed the stop button. "You will not run alone for two weeks." He gave me a stern look. "And if there is any discomfort, you stop immediately."

"Yes, sir." I said and he nodded before heading for the door. I watched him go and immediately missed his comforting presence. Once the door closed, I looked back at the guys. "I really am sorry. I thought you were right behind me."

Mike scoffed. "Do you know how fast you run? I don't think anyone could catch you."

I pressed the button on the machine and put one earbud in so that I could still hear the guys if they spoke to me. My sore muscles screamed in protest, but I pushed past it. Over the next ten minutes, I slowly increased the speed until I was almost sprinting. This was my thinking speed. Another ten minutes ticked by before anyone talked.

"My dad seems to really like you." Easton said from beside me.

I glanced over at him. "Your dad is seriously a great guy." I said without missing a beat. "It's nice to know that he thinks of me as a daughter, because he is like a father to me." I took a sip from my water bottle before putting it back in the cup holder. "For some reason your parents have taken me under their wing. I don't get it, but I love them for it."

Easton watched me for several minutes before walking away. I got back into my head and relived the fight with Jet. What was the point of it all? Something was off about the whole thing and why did he look familiar?

My mind wandered to mom's reaction to Jet and her overprotective behavior today. I have never seen her lose her temper and we have been through a lot over the years. Then there was the whole conversation with the Alpha and Jason.

"Carly Brooks!" My mother's scream caused me to jump and trip.

The treadmill pulled my feet out from under me, but before I fell, arms wrapped around me and yanked me away from the moving belt. My rescuer and I landed hard on the ground and rolled twice before stopping. I looked to see who saved me from falling and getting road rash only to come face-to-face with Easton.

He was on his back with me laying on his chest. One arm was around my waist while the other cradled the back of my head. We were both breathing hard, and I dropped my head back down on his chest to try to catch my breath. I pulled my earbud out as I continued to lay there. Cora laughed and told me I should run with Easton more.

"Holy crap!" Max rushed over and put his hand on my back. "Are you okay, Carly?"

"What were you thinking, Carly?" My mother yelled as she approached. "You should be at home, resting."

I groaned and rolled off Easton, his arm getting trapped under me, but I didn't care. My heart was beating so hard, it felt like it was going to burst from my chest. I stared at the ceiling as mom continued to scold me for not being careful, and how I could have been seriously hurt if Easton hadn't been there to catch me when I fell. I wanted to tell her that I wouldn't have fallen if she hadn't scared me, but I bit my tongue.

"Mrs. Brooks, would you like us to take Carly back to your house since you said you have to get back to work?" Max interjected quickly when mom stopped her rant to take a breath.

Mom paused for a second. "Yes, that would be good. I trust that you gentlemen can make sure she stays at the house this time." The guys all told her, yes, and mom left as quickly as she had come.

"Thanks for the save." I sat up and looked at them. "For the near fall and my mom." I sighed and got to my feet, moving over to my clothes. I took off my shoes and pulled on the sweatpants and hoodie. "She can be crazy overprotective." I shoved my shoes in my bag and zipped it closed before heading for the door.

"Why aren't you wearing shoes?" Max asked.

"I can't wear these shoes outside; they are strictly for the gym." I glanced over at him. "And if we are fast enough, my feet won't even feel the cold on the way home."

Easton grabbed my hand and pulled me to a stop just before we got to the side door. "I don't think so. Mike, can you carry the bag?" Mike took my bag with a smile. I looked between the three of them confused. Easton swept me up into his arms and I squeaked in surprise, which only made them laugh.

"Put me down, Easton." I said as I tried to struggle in his grip, but my battered body refused to put any real strength behind it.

"Not a chance. You were nearly a popsicle, beaten, sprinted for over an hour, and fell off a treadmill. I am not letting you walk home barefoot in the dark." Easton stated with a smirk. "Plus, your mom just told us to make sure you got home to rest. If you take off on us again, your mom and my dad will have our heads."

He had a point, and if I walked home without shoes on, I could get sick. Cora pointed out that I was already sick, but I ignored her. I sighed in resignation and folded my arms over my chest. I was hyper aware of every movement Easton made as we walked back to my house. I was glad it was dark because my face burned as I remembered Easton with his shirt off, all of his muscles, and the feel of his arms around me when he had saved me from falling.

I was both relieved and disappointed to see my house coming into view. Easton deposited me on the couch once we were inside, but I felt energetic. Whenever I was near Easton lately, I gained a new sense of energy.

I stood and moved into the kitchen with my three shadows tagging along. "What do you guys want to eat?" I asked as I opened the fridge.

"You are supposed to be resting." Easton reminded me.

"Cooking can be considered resting." I countered as I pulled items out of the fridge. "You're in luck guys, we have a few steaks that need to be eaten." I said with a smile.

We had only three steaks, but I could cut them up to make them go farther. All three of the guys were watching me from the table and I grew self-conscious. In an effort to ignore them, I turned on the radio much louder than I normally would and began to cook fajitas. I was along with the music when I remembered I was under house arrest and my guards were in the room. I glanced over at them and saw that they were playing cards.

Dinner was ready and I dished up five plates. I stuck one in the microwave, for when Mom got home, and took the other four to the table. The guys raved about the food as I ate quietly. I smiled and thanked them for the compliments. I was starting to feel worse by the minute.

Once I was done, I cleared and washed the dishes. Without looking at the guys, I went upstairs and took a quick shower. After taking some Tylenol and blow drying my hair, I crawled into bed, feeling completely exhausted.

Tomorrow was school and I would have to face Marissa and the rest of the student body. Chances were, everyone knew about the trial and about my sparring match with Jet. I heard someone knock on my doorframe, but I rolled over, so my back was facing the door.

"They are trying to help, and you are making them worry." Cora chastised me.

"I'm tired and I just want to sleep. I can't sleep knowing they are in my room." I told her.

She scoffed. *"That didn't stop you before."*

I rolled my eyes. "Good night, Cora." I sighed.

Chapter 7

I woke up with a start and immediately scanned my room. I was completely alone. I shook my head and smiled as I got out of bed. I was feeling much better than the night before. I stretched and flexed my elbow. No pain. I moved into my bathroom and took a quick shower. I brushed my hair before braiding it. As I dried off, I took stock of the bruises on my body.

I was a complete mess. My ribs on the left side were black and blue. My elbow had some bruising on it as well, but no swelling. Long fingerlike bruises wrapped around my wrists where Jet had grabbed me. I hadn't thought about putting the cream on them yesterday.

"At least you don't have to deal with the pain that should accompany such injuries." Cora commented. "It looks so bad."

"We are lucky we had the witch's cream. I can't even imagine the level of pain this would have caused." I told her. "Come on, we have school to get ready for."

I wrapped the towel around myself and headed for my closet. My bedroom door was open, but that wasn't anything new. With only Mom and me in the house, we rarely closed our doors, even when we dressed.

I pulled on clean underwear and a bra before I looked through my clothes. I grabbed a pair of jeans and a green long sleeve shirt to change into after I put on an undershirt and workout shorts. My room wasn't the most well organized. My things weren't at all put together with similar items. My clothes were located in three different areas. Mom and Cora teased me about it constantly, but I didn't care. I liked having my workout clothes close to the bathroom, since I layered them under my normal clothes.

I tossed my towel towards my computer chair as I stepped out of the closet. I let out a startled yelp when I saw Easton sitting in the chair as he caught the towel. I felt my cheeks flush as we stared at each other. Both of us were frozen in surprise. Cora's laughter finally snapped me out of my shock at seeing Easton in my room.

"Get out!" I yelled, trying to use my folded clothes as some sort of cover. Before he could move, Max burst into my room. He quickly looked around, his eyes settling on me. "Both of you get out!" I yelled, Easton and Max ran from the room, slamming the door behind them.

"What were they doing in here?" I asked Cora.

"Beats me." Cora shrugged. *"I suggest we get dressed quickly and then go downstairs to see what they were thinking."* Cora suggested, sounding just as upset as I was.

I decided to forego my light makeup and got dressed as fast as possible. The longer I was in my room, the more frustrated and embarrassed I got. I opened my door and started for the stairs, but stopped before descending when I heard Max and Easton talking in the front room.

"She looked ticked." Max said quietly.

"Carly has every right to be angry with us." Easton said with a sigh. "I had no idea she didn't have clothes on. The door was wide open for crying out loud."

"I'm sure she will understand when we tell her we had no idea she would be so...undressed." Max tried to sound confident, but the uncertainty in his voice made him only sound worried. "I had no idea she had that kind of body. She looked amazing when we saw her spar against Jet, but those sculpted legs," He let out a whistle. "And I never thought she would be into lace."

My face burned. Easton growled and Max laughed. I decided to end the conversation by walking down the stairs. They heard me and the tension in the room was so thick I could have cut it with a spoon. I glared at them as I walked past and headed for the kitchen. They hesitated before following me. Mom was in the kitchen cooking. She looked up and smiled when I walked into the room.

"Oh good, you're up. I sent Mr. Shepherd upstairs to let you know that breakfast was ready." Mom set a plate on the table for me. "Are you still hurting? I thought I heard you yell."

"No, Mom. I'm fine." I ground out. "I'm not really hungry." She gave me a strange look but glanced over at the doorway. I followed her gaze.

Easton and Max stood awkwardly with red faces. "I'm sure they will love to eat." I gave mom a hug and kiss. "I need to make sure I have everything for midterms." I shouldered past Easton and went upstairs to grab my school bag. They were all still in the kitchen when I got back downstairs. "See you tonight, Mom. I love you." I called down the hall as I opened up the door and slammed it behind me.

I walked fast heading towards the school. It was a twenty-minute walk, but I often jogged it, cutting the time down. Today, however, I decided I needed a few extra minutes of solitude before reaching the school. Running footsteps behind me caused me to grind my teeth in frustration. I didn't need to turn around to know that Easton and Max were following me.

"At least she isn't running." Max muttered quietly.

I growled as I turned around to face them. I jammed my finger into Max's chest as I spoke. He threw his hands up in a show of surrender. "You don't get to make jokes right now. You don't get to speak to me, and I sure as heck, don't want you looking at me. Do I make myself clear?" Max nodded before I turned around and started walking again.

"You can be quite intimidating when you want to be." Cora laughed.

"My legs, seriously?" I muttered to her.

"You heard that?" Max sounded mortified and I realized I had spoken out loud.

I wrapped my arms around myself and continued to school, trying to ignore the fact that they were behind me. As soon as we got into the halls, I ducked low and slipped into one of my old hiding places. They were looking around at the students and passed by without seeing me.

I had been right, there was lots of talk about the trial. To my relief, there was no mention of me and Jet sparring. I made it all the way to lunch without crossing paths with Mike, Max, or Easton. I was currently hiding in one of the girls' bathrooms. I was sitting on the toilet lid with my legs up when a couple of girls entered.

"I can't believe Easton Shepherd defended you during the trial." Mariah, one of Marissa's friends, was saying.

"I'm telling you; he was the one that changed the council's minds on my punishment. I thought he liked me, but that just confirmed it." Marissa sighed dreamily.

"What about finding your mate?" Mariah asked.

"I don't care about my mate. All I want is Easton. Wolves choose their mates all the time these days." Marissa said as she laughed. "I will be Easton Shepherd's chosen mate, you'll see."

My stomach tightened at the very thought of Marissa and Easton. Which was ridiculous because he wasn't mine to be possessive over. They continued talking about Easton, and Marissa's plans to secure him. I became nauseous as they carried on. The bell rang and they finally left.

I waited another minute before I slowly made my way out to the hall. I needed to hurry so I could get to class. My stomach churned with unease as I walked down the hall with my head down. A noise in the hall to my left caused me to turn my head to see what was there. Marissa had her arms around Easton's neck and his hands were on her hips. She giggled at something he said, and I felt sick. I quickly walked past, hoping that neither of them saw me.

"What does she think she is doing?" Cora growled. *"She has no right to be touching him."*

"He didn't seem too upset by the attention." I told her, even though I felt like I was punched in the gut. *"Easton can make his own decisions. If he doesn't want to find his mate, then he doesn't have to."*

"The mate bond is sacred." Cora fumed.

She was right, the bond between mates was special and irreplaceable. We both had strong feelings about mates. That is why I had not bothered even paying attention to boys. I was waiting until my eighteenth birthday so I could find my mate. I didn't want to be emotionally involved with someone, only to have to walk away when I found my mate. It wouldn't be fair to any of us.

"It has nothing to do with us, Cora. Now stop getting worked up about this, we have one more midterm we need to focus on." I told her as I turned down the hall and collided with someone.

"There you are." Mike said. "We have been looking all over for you."

"Wish I could talk, but I have a test I'm late for." I shouldered past him, and he sighed. I opened the door to the science room and stepped in.

Disappointment shone in my teacher's eyes as he looked at me and commented on me being late. I apologized and sat quickly. He dropped my test in front of me before moving back to his desk. I immediately began.

It took me two hours to complete the test. I rubbed a hand over my face as I sat back. Glancing up at the clock, I realized I had missed most of sparring class. Not that I was complaining, I would have just been studying anyway. I rose from my chair and handed in my test. I gathered my things and exited the classroom. Max stood leaning against the wall when I looked up, and I groaned.

"What do you want?" I snapped at him. The halls were thankfully empty at the moment.

"I am sorry, Carr. I heard you scream and ran up to see what had happened." A blush rose up his neck and into his cheeks. "And I'm sorry for saying those things about you."

I glared at him. I understood the accident of him coming in on me. Easton however, had just been hanging out in my room while I was getting dressed. That was not okay. I turned away from him without saying anything and headed for the front doors. Sparring was my last class of the day, and since it was already halfway over, I wasn't going to stay.

Max was right behind me all the way. Once outside, he grabbed my elbow to stop me. I yanked myself from his grip and took off running. I heard him curse, but I didn't turn to see if he followed. I took the forest path, and at the fork I veered in the direction of the waterfall. I needed to clear my head.

I threw my bag on the shore before I took my sweatshirt and shoes off. I dove into the deep end. The shock of the cold water caused me to push to the surface quickly and take in a gasping breath. With chattering teeth, I swam towards the falls. I dove under the base of the waterfall, coming up on the back side.

I climbed up the slippery rock wall until I reached a small cave about ten feet up. I pulled myself inside and laid there shivering. I laid there for a good fifteen minutes watching the forest through the distortion of the falling water. An odd movement caught my attention.

"Cora, is that...?" I asked.

"That is definitely a person." She confirmed.

"Why can't they just leave me alone?" I yelled inside my head.

I laid there as still as I could while shivering. I became confused as the person was joined by several more. I looked at them more closely. Even with the water distorting details, I could tell that none of the people were Easton, Max, or Mike. They moved differently. One of the figures bent down near the shore and I realized he was digging through my backpack.

Four more figures joined the others, and I recognized them immediately. There seemed to be an argument before the first group left. The one I suspected was Easton, picked up my bag that the other man had been messing with. The roar of the falls made it impossible to hear anything.

Easton, Max, Mike, and, it looked like Jason, spread out around the waterfall. I scooted to the edge of the cave and sucked in my breath, then jumped. Pushing off the bottom of the pool I angled towards the shore. I broke the surface and looked around.

"I told you she was freaking crazy!" Max yelled. I walked out of the pool and headed for the path without giving any of them a second glance.

My arm was grabbed, and I was spun around. Jason stood there with a hard expression. "What has gotten into you, Carr?" he asked angrily. I wrapped my arms around myself and stood there shivering, waiting for him to continue his lecture. "Answer me, Carly. What is going on?"

"I just n-needed to think." My teeth were chattering. "Then there w-were those g-guys. I s-stayed out of s-sight. W-what d-did they w-want anyw-way?" I asked.

Jason sighed and wrapped his arms around me. His warmth was amazing. "Dax is claiming you are his mate. He wants us to hand you over to him."

I stepped away from Jason. "No, w-way." I said and began walking. "T-that guy is n-not my m-mate." I fumed.

"*He could be.*" Cora said slowly. "*He does seem awfully keen on us. Maybe he* really *is our mate.*"

"He accused Easton of being our mate at the beginning. If he were our mate, he wouldn't have said something like that." I argued. "*Just a few more weeks and we will know for sure and then we can figure out what to do. Because I am not staying with a guy like him.*"

"Your birthday is in a few months. You will know then." Jason said. "Until then, I don't want you going to the falls alone."

"I c-can't run alone. I can't g-go to the f-falls alone. I am b-beginning to think I c-can't even get d-dressed alone." I growled out. "If y-you are going to p-put me under h-house arrest J-Jason, just c-call it what it is."

"Carr, we are just trying to keep you safe. And what is with this fight in you? You usually just go with the flow." Jason asked. He looked curious, not mad. I, on the other hand, was getting mad.

My house came into view, and I stopped on the porch to look at Jason. Easton, Mike, and Max were standing behind him wearing looks of concern.

"I have always been this w-way. I am just tired of rolling over and t-taking all the crap that others deal me. I'm t-tired of running and hiding. I'm tired of f-feeling weak all the time. S-seriously, what other w-wolf gets this cold?" I was shivering uncontrollably. "If D-Dax is my m-mate, then he can s-shove it, because there is no w-way I would ever be with a b-bully like him." I went inside, slammed the door, and locked it.

Once in my room, I closed and locked my door as well, before going into the bathroom. I needed to get in a warm shower before I did anything else.

I got out and dressed into my warmest clothes. I started to climb into my bed, but stopped when I heard my cell phone go off in the hallway. I opened my door slowly. My bag and shoes were sitting on the floor next to my door. I grabbed them before returning to my bed. I fished out my phone and looked at it.

Mom sent me a text saying she was having the nice boys stay at the house until she got home, because she wasn't expected back until late. I rolled my eyes as I snuggled deeper under the covers. I was still shivering, which did not bode well. I hadn't been feeling particularly well since the trial. The stresses over the last week were finally catching up to me.

There was another message, this one from Jason. He was reassuring me that Dax wouldn't be able to take me without my permission, and that he was sorry if he ever made me feel like I couldn't be myself around him. He also asked me to call him when I was feeling up to it. I just wanted to be left alone for a while. I closed my eyes and allowed myself to relax.

Chapter 8

My alarm woke me up and I opened my eyes slowly as I looked around. I sighed when I noticed that I was blessedly alone. I forced myself out of bed, still feeling chilled. I dragged my feet as I made my way to the bathroom and jumped into a hot shower. It didn't help.

My muscles were achy, and I had a slight headache. I got back into my warm clothes and grabbed my bag. I half expected to see one or all the guys in the living room, but it was empty too. I smiled when I saw that my mom was the only person in the kitchen. I opened up the bread box on the counter and took out a slice. I wasn't feeling particularly hungry, but knew I needed to eat something.

"How does it feel to only have nine weeks left until you graduate?" Mom smiled at me.

"I cannot wait for it to be over. I hate school." Mom laughed as she took a sip of her coffee. "You seem rather happy this morning." I observed.

"I am off until Friday." she said with a shrug. I scrunched my brows together; mom never got weekdays off. When she saw my confused look, her smile fell, and she sighed. "I am going with Beta Harry and his wife to a couple neighboring packs. We will be gone for two weeks."

"Since when do you take assignments outside of the pack?" I asked. Mom had never left me alone before and I wasn't sure how I felt about it.

"You are nearly an adult, Carly, even if the pack believes you still have several more months to go. I trust you to be able to hold down the fort until I get back." She walked over to me and gave me a hug. "I have asked Gamma Jason and Gamma Holly to look in on you from time to time." I nodded, still feeling confused as to why she had to go. "I would have turned down the assignment if I could have, especially with it being so close to your birthday and first shift, but I couldn't. If for some reason I am unable to get back in time for your shift, lock the doors, close all the windows, and go to the basement. Shift there."

I looked at her and I could see that this was hard for her, too. "I will be fine. Don't worry." I told her with a forced smile, hoping to relieve some of her concerns.

We talked for a few more minutes before she ushered me out the door to head to school. I puzzled over mom's upcoming absence and was absorbed in my own thoughts. Someone bumped into me, and I was surprised when I found myself already in front of the school. I looked at the person I had collided with and inwardly groaned.

"Hi, Marissa." I said as pleasantly as I could.

If looks could kill, I would have been six feet under. She took a threatening step towards me as she glanced around. "Stay away from him." Her voice was so low that only I could hear her. "Easton is mine. Do you understand?" She was practically snarling.

I took a step back to avoid our noses touching. "I have no intention of taking someone else's mate, Marissa." I kept my voice equally low. "I value the mate bond." Marissa's eyes widened slightly, as I stepped towards her. "I don't plan on having a relationship with anyone but my mate." I bumped my shoulder against hers as I brushed past her.

"That's my girl!" Cora cheered. *"Marissa could not believe that you actually stood up to her. You are a rock star."*

"Thanks, Cora. It did feel kind of good to stand up for myself." I admitted as I sat down in my chair in my first class.

The day dragged on, and I was freezing. The cold was bone deep, and I got several odd looks from other students when they saw me shiver. This wasn't good. I could practically feel the sickness coming on.

I passed Max and Mike in the hall a few times and they gave me friendly smiles, but there was something in their eyes that told me something was wrong. I tried to ignore it, but when the same look appeared in Gamma Holly's expression during Sparring class, I couldn't help but feel concerned as well. What worried them?

I was heading home when Mike walked up to me with a smile. "Mind if I walk with you? My dad asked if I could give your mom some documents." He held up a packet of papers as proof.

Glancing over at him, I shrugged. "Sure." I forced a smile before continuing toward my house.

Mike talked almost constantly as we walked. I only had to input a word here or there, which suited me just fine. When we stepped into my house, mom came out of the kitchen with a smile.

"I have a lot of homework. I'm going to head to my room to work on it." I excused myself and went straight upstairs.

The rest of the day passed in a blur. I did my homework on autopilot, ate dinner with mom, then fell into bed completely exhausted.

The next two days followed a similar pattern with the exception of developing a fever. I forced myself out of bed and spent a few minutes talking with mom with as much cheer as I could muster, before heading to school. I sat quietly in classes, pushed my food around on my plate during lunch and slept during Sparring class. Either Mike or Max would give some excuse and walk me home. I felt too crappy to call them out on their ridiculous excuses and just let them. I saw Easton at a distance a few times. He didn't seem to notice me, but he looked beyond stressed. According to the kids in his classes, he was irritable, and class was brutal.

Thursday came and the school day dragged by slowly. I felt like crap and all I wanted to do was go home and sleep for a week. I sighed in relief when I stepped outside to head home. Mom would be gone in the morning, and I planned to call in sick on Friday so I could sleep the whole day.

"Hey." Easton's voice at my side caused me to jump.

"Hey." I said with a small smile. I hadn't talked to him since he saw me getting dressed and I had been feeling anxious to talk with him again.

"Would it be okay if I…?" His voice trailed off as he glanced in the direction of my house. I nodded and we started walking. We walked for a few minutes in silence. "I'm sorry for…" He started to say but stopped.

"It's water under the bridge, Easton." I said softly. He let out a tense breath and his whole demeanor relaxed. I was fighting the urge to just lay down where I was. I was so tired, but I kept telling myself to take one more step. Just one more, and as soon as I got home, I could sleep.

"Are you doing okay?" He asked turning to study me.

"I'm doing fine." I said tiredly.

"Liar." Cora scoffed. *"And you are not very good at it. You haven't been this sick in years."*

"You are a terrible liar." Easton said.

I laughed. "Cora said the same thing."

"Who's Cora?" Easton asked, grabbing my arm gently and pulling me to a stop. I shivered and Easton pulled me to him as he put his arms around me. "Why are you shivering when you feel so warm?" he asked with concern.

I leaned against him and took a moment to relish the warmth that spread throughout my body. "Cora, is my wolf." I mumbled against his chest.

Easton's body tensed and he pulled back enough to look down at me. "Your wolf? You've shifted?"

I blinked up at him. Why would he ask me about my wolf when everyone still thought I had months till my birthday? "My wolf?" I repeated, confused.

"You said Cora is your wolf." he said as his brows drew together. "Carr, are you feeling okay?"

I shook my head and leaned back against him. "I'm so tired." I whispered as I closed my eyes.

"Hey Carr, stay awake for me." Easton said anxiously as his arms tightened around me. "Hey man. Get Max and my dad and meet me at Carly's house. Something is wrong with her." Easton shifted slightly before his hand touched my face. "You still with me, Carly?" His voice was soft and soothing.

"I just want to lay down, East." I said as I tried to sit down. I just needed to rest for a minute. Easton tightened his hold on me, preventing me from sinking to the ground. I didn't have the energy to protest when he picked me up and started walking.

Before I knew it, I was set on the couch and Easton's warmth went away. "Hey." I protested.

"Look at me, Carr." Easton demanded as he touched my face. I blinked and my eyes focused on him. "You feel like a furnace. What do you need?" He asked.

"You need to get warm." Cora said. *"You are shivering."*

"I think I have a fever." I told her and Easton looked at me with even more concern.

"Take some Tylenol and then snuggle under something warm. I hate to see you shivering." Cora said as she paced. *"Hopefully when we shift, this won't happen again."*

"That would be nice." I said as I blinked my eyes slowly.

The corner of Easton's mouth quirked up. "What would be nice?" he asked as he stroked my cheek with his thumb.

I looked at him and blinked a few times. I shook my head to try to clear it. I was having a hard time thinking. I just wanted sleep. "She said when we shift, I might not get sick anymore." I mumbled. Easton studied my face for a minute before sitting on the couch next to me. He put his arm around my shoulders, and I snuggled into his side. "You're so warm." I said softly and I felt Easton chuckle.

Lowered voices woke me. I snuggled into my pillow just wanting a few more minutes of sleep. My pillow moved. I bolted upright and a wave of dizziness caused my vision to tilt. I grabbed my head in my hands and leaned forward until my head was between my knees.

A hand touched my back. When the dizziness passed, I slowly sat up. I jumped when I saw Gamma Jason, Mike, and Max standing around my living room while Easton sat next to me on the couch.

"What?" I rubbed a hand down my face. "Why are...?" I shook my head. "What is going on?" I finally managed to say. I still felt like I was burning up, yet I was freezing. My muscles ached and I was so tired.

I stood and slowly made my way into the kitchen. I needed to take something to bring my fever down. Mom was not going to be happy that I was sick again.

"Carr, what are you doing?" Jason asked from the kitchen doorway. "What can I get for you?"

I pulled open the medicine cabinet and started pulling out bottles as I looked for the ones I wanted. "Where is my mom?" I asked.

"What are all those?" Max asked as he walked up beside me. He grabbed one of the bottles and looked at it. "Loratadine. Seriously, what are these?"

I rolled my eyes as I undid the cap of the Tylenol and shook out two pills. "These are called medications." I said as if I was talking to a child. I opened the ibuprofen next and shook out two more pills. "Humans use them to help with all sorts of illnesses. Like fever, cramps, colds, the flu, and allergies. Things you normal wolves never have to worry about." I filled a glass of water and swallowed the pills before turning around. I was so tired. I lowered myself to the ground before looking up. "Hopefully, in an hour, my fever will start going down."

"Why don't we get you off the floor and back into the living room where we can talk." Jason said as he crouched next to me. He picked me up and carried me into the other room, placing me back on the couch. "Now, sweetheart, your mom had to leave early on her trip." Jason told me as he watched my face.

"Good." I breathed out. "She gets way too worried when I get sick."

"Sorry to break it to you, but I think we are all worried about you at this point." Easton said as he sat down next to me. "You practically passed out on the walk back from the school and you weren't making any sense."

"What are you talking about?" I asked as I pulled a blanket off the back of the couch and put it over my legs.

"You said Cora was your wolf and when you shift, you both hoped that you wouldn't get sick anymore." I looked over at Easton with wide eyes. I glanced around the room, and everyone was watching me closely.

"Did I...?" I asked Cora.

"I'm afraid so." she said softly. *"You were also talking to me but saying things out loud."*

"What are the odds I can blame it on the fever?" I asked her.

"I don't think Jason would believe you."

I covered my face with my hands and leaned my head back against the couch. "This can't be happening." I groaned. I took several deep breaths to calm myself. I was pretty sure they could all hear my frantically beating heart. I finally lowered my hands and looked around at everyone in the room before lowering my gaze to my hands. "What are the odds of you guys letting me rest for a few hours before we have this talk?" I looked pleadingly at Jason.

He studied my face for a few minutes before slowly nodding. "You do look pale. Easton and Mike will stay with you for now and I will be back later tonight."

"I will be fine without babysitters." I said, crossing my arms.

Jason gave me a dubious look. "If you want, I can take you to the pack hospital instead."

"Babysitters it is, Papa Bear." I said quickly and he smiled.

"Papa Bear?" Max asked with a laugh.

I nodded before laying my head down on the arm of the couch. "He is almost as bad as a mama bear protecting her cub." I yawned. All the guys laughed at that.

"Get some rest, little cub." Jason placed a kiss on my head before he and Max left. The room fell blessedly quiet, and I sighed.

I shifted to get more comfortable. The couch was small and with Easton sitting next to me, there wasn't any room for me to pull my feet up. Easton grabbed my legs and laid them over his lap. I looked at him in surprise and tried to pull my legs away, but he held them in place. He raised his brow in challenge, and I gave up. I didn't have the strength to fight him. I settled more comfortably and closed my eyes again. The TV clicked on as my body began to relax. The whistle of a sports game was the last thing I remember hearing.

Chapter 9

"Is Dax really claiming Carly is his mate?" Mike's voice asked quietly.

"Dax is a prick." I grumbled.

"But he does have gorgeous blue eyes and he looks like he has an amazing physique." Cora interjected. *"But I think I find Easton way cuter."*

"You're awake." Mike said in surprise. I pulled my legs off Easton's lap and slowly sat up.

"How are you feeling?" Easton asked as he laid my blanket over my lap.

"Like I'm sick." I grumbled. "How long have I been out?"

"Almost five hours." Easton studied me. "I thought those pills you took were supposed to make you better?"

"They reduce the fever for only four to six hours." I corrected.

"Hey Max, bring in some of those pills Carly took earlier and a glass of water." Mike called loudly and I glared at him. My head was aching, and his yelling wasn't helping anything. "I don't think I have ever seen you grumpy."

"You try having a fever, body aches, a pounding headache, and absolutely no energy. See if you feel a little 'grumpy'." I pulled the blanket closer. "And I'm still cold."

A minute later, Max appeared in the doorway with two pill bottles, a cup of water, and a stack of sandwiches. "Would you like me to make you one?" he asked. I shook my head as he handed me the bottles. Max handed Mike a sandwich while I quickly downed the meds.

When he handed Easton his, I grabbed it and took a bite before handing it over to Easton. "Thanks." Easton said sarcastically.

"Sorry." I said around my mouthful as they all stared at me. I swallowed and followed it with another drink of water. "I needed to eat something with the ibuprofen otherwise it upsets my stomach."

"I can go make you one." Max said again as he laughed.

"But I don't want one." I whined. Easton shook his head and took a bite of his sandwich.

"So, what makes you not like Dax?" Mike asked.

"He is a liar for starters, even though he is gorgeous. His eyes, his strong jaw, the way his shirt hugged him. Mmm." Cora said, causing me to chuckle and shake my head.

"What's so funny about that question?" Max asked curiously.

"Not the question, Cora's response to the question." I smiled as I closed my eyes and rested my head against the back of the couch. "She was listing off a few of Dax's good qualities with one of his obvious flaws."

It was quiet so long that I peeked at the guys. "Good qualities?" Mike asked in disbelief.

"He has amazing eyes and a body that is impossible not to appreciate." I said without thinking much of it. "But he is a liar and manipulator, which makes it hard to admire those better qualities for long."

"You think Dax is hot?" Max roared with laughter.

"Easton is hot. Dax is attractive." Cora clarified.

"Cora sure thinks he is cute." I smirked at him. "And like you have room to talk. You have a thing for well-toned legs and lace." I shot back at him, and his face turned crimson. "Plus, Dax is not my type."

"Wait, what?" Mike looked between us. "Lace? How do you know Max likes lace?"

"Max and…" I started to say, and Max cut me off.

"It was an accident, Carr."

"You have said that the guys at the school aren't your type before. What does that even mean?" Easton asked seriously. His own face had gone as red as Max's. "You just admitted you find Dax attractive."

"Correction, I find his eyes attractive. Cora likes his strong jaw and ample muscles." I said with a shrug. "A girl can find certain aspects of a guy attractive without actually wanting to be with the guy. I can usually find something to like about any guy and still not want anything to do with him. Dax is no exception. Sure, his eyes are a beautiful shade of blue, but I also want to shove him off a cliff."

Max laughed. "That is a bit extreme."

"Is it?" I asked. "The guy is claiming I am his mate, which I am not, knowing full well that I personally cannot deny it since I am not eighteen and haven't shifted. He has mentioned several times that he wants me to go back to his pack with him, even though I made it pretty clear that I'm not going anywhere with him the last time we met."

"Since you can't know for certain that he is not your mate yet, why do you think he is lying?" Mike asked.

"I don't think; I know." I crossed my arms over my chest. "The first time I met him, he called me 'mystery girl' then accused Max or Easton of being my mate. If he were my mate, he would have worded it differently."

"What do you mean?" Easton asked.

"He said, 'what? are you her mate or something?' I'm sorry, but I don't see a man saying something like that when some guy puts his shirt on the first man's mate. He would have gotten possessive and protective and said something more like 'what, you think she is *your* mate?'. There is a huge difference." I explained. "He called you my mate and told me to let him show me how a real man treats a woman. Then pulled the whole Gamma vs Alpha card." I shook my head. "I don't buy this mate ploy of his."

"She has a point. I would have been livid if I saw some guy put his shirt on my mate." Max leaned back in his chair. "My question is, you have your wolf, so why can't you tell who your mate is?"

"That is a complicated story. I think we should wait for Papa Bear." I said tiredly.

The front door opened and closed. As if I had conjured him just by speaking about him, Gamma Jason walked into the room followed by Gamma Holly. He smiled when he saw me sitting up. "You look a little better." He said with a small nod.

"That is a little better? Oh, you poor dear." Gamma Holly rushed over and gave me a hug. "Jason told me that you weren't feeling well. I insisted on coming to help take care of you until tomorrow."

"Thank you." I smiled at her.

"I'm going to look in the kitchen and see if I can make you something." Holly hurried from the room and Max chuckled.

"I'm her son and didn't even get a hello." Easton complained. "Even mom likes you better." He scowled playfully at me. He turned to his dad. "She is still calling you Papa Bear, by the way."

Easton waved his hand with his sandwich in my direction, and I grabbed it from him. I took another bite and gave it back. He looked at me surprised. "Last time, I promise." I said covering my mouth with my hand as I chewed. While keeping eye contact with me, he shoved the last two bites of the sandwich in his mouth.

"What were you all talking about when we got here?" Jason asked as he took a seat in mom's chair, there was a spark of humor in his eyes.

"Carly was just about to tell us how she has her wolf before she is eighteen." Max said with an eager expression.

"Honestly, I don't know. I was sixteen when Cora first spoke to me." I ran my hand through my hair. "I can't see her in my mind, but I know what she is feeling and can tell when she is pacing or just relaxing. We can't shift and we don't have any of our wolf senses. Cora says she won't be able to sense our mate until we shift, but she doesn't know why we can communicate without her fully being a part of me."

"What does your mom have to say about this?" Jason asked.

"She doesn't know. No one knew until the stupid fever muddled my brain." I looked down at my hands.

"But you know your wolf's personality?" Easton asked.

"I am the best part of you. I would rule this pack if I were more in charge." Cora laughed.

A smile tugged at my lips. "Cora is feisty and always ready for a fight. We both love to run. When I run, it's like she is too. It's kinda hard to explain. When I'm cold, she can feel the cold as well. She loves practical jokes and having a good laugh. And she is insanely loyal."

"So, she is pretty much you." Jason said with a smile. "Do you have many differences?"

I thought about that for a minute. *"How we see and interact with attractive men. For example, I am all for snuggling close to Easton, while you are shyer and more reserved."* Cora interjected.

"I'm not saying that." I told her as I felt my cheeks heat.

"Oh, this has got to be good. What did your wolf say?" Max rubbed his hands together.

I sent him a glare. "All I'm going to say is that she is bolder than I am. More willing to be seen."

"According to your records, you turn eighteen in a few months." Jason said thoughtfully. "But our problem with Dax is now. He is trying to get the council to agree to move you to his pack. He claims that as your mate, he should be close to you."

"As my mate, he shouldn't be making such a claim. Isn't it against the ancient laws to tell one's mate who you are to them before they have shifted?" I asked.

"Yes and no. Since your age gap is small, he is arguing that you are so close enough to your shift that it shouldn't matter. He has pointed out that there are some regions farther south where werewolves can shift as young as sixteen." Jason glanced over at Easton. "He is also arguing that you three are messing with Carly's head and confusing her about who her real mate is."

"That's ridiculous." I said as I laid back down. "As soon as I shift, I would be able to feel the bond with him if he were my mate." I pulled the blanket more over my shoulders. Easton once again lifted my legs and put them across his lap. "Not that it matters, if Dax is my mate, I am rejecting him."

"Carly is right about Dax's earlier behavior; he never has acted like a jealous or possessive mate." Max commented.

"He claimed that while on patrol at the neighboring pack's border, he could smell her while she was at the waterfall." Easton shook his head. "It doesn't make sense. Even for a mate, that is too big of a distance to smell one another." He tensed and slowly turned to study me. "But not for a tracker." He said slowly.

"You think Dax was sent here to track me?" I asked in shock. "Why would anyone want to track me? I am a nobody." I looked around the room.

"You might be onto something, East." Jason rubbed his jaw. "Carly, whatever brought you and your mother here all those years ago may have found you."

I looked at Jason and swallowed. I wasn't even sure what we were running from. Mom had never wanted to talk about it. Could Dax be a tracker sent to collect mom and me? A tense silence filled the room. Holly came in with a smile, but it fell when she saw everyone's expressions. Jason filled her in on Easton's theory and she began pacing.

"I will stay with you tonight. But we all have things we need to do tomorrow, and I don't think you are well enough to go to school." Holly turned to look at me with worry in her eyes.

"I will be fine. I'll lock the doors and send regular updates to Papa Bear if it makes you feel better." I said. "I really don't think Dax will come this far into pack lands just to try to get to me."

"You call Jason, Papa Bear?" Holly laughed despite the tension in the room. "Is that why you have been referring to her as Cub?" She asked Jason.

He only smiled over at me and winked, causing Holly to laugh. "After school, one of the guys will sit with you until I can come back over in the evening. I will set up a schedule for the weekend so that you are never alone."

I tried to protest but both Holly and Jason refused to back down. I finally relented and rolled on my back. I was staring at the ceiling as I started to doze off. I gasped when Easton picked me up and headed for the stairs. "Easy, Carr. I'm just taking you up to your bed so you will be more comfortable during the night." He whispered close to my ear.

"Just don't drop me." I whispered back as I put my arm around his shoulders.

Easton's arms tightened around me, holding me closer to him. "I will never drop you." The seriousness in his tone had me turning to look at him. We were so close that my nose brushed against his jaw. He looked down at me and our lips almost touched. Heat radiated between us, and I was sure that he was going to kiss me.

"I got the pillow." Max said from behind us, breaking whatever spell we had been trapped in.

Easton took the last remaining steps to my bed quickly before setting me down gently. He tucked me in, and I thanked both him and Max for their help. Easton gave me a small smile while Max saluted before they left. The quiet of the room had me feeling completely alone. It was weird, I was left alone for long periods of time while mom worked, but for some reason, I felt abandoned.

Chapter 10

Papa Bear had taken me giving him an update every hour very seriously. I had fallen asleep and must have rolled onto my phone. The next thing I knew, my door was thrown off its hinges and a very worried looking Gamma Jason stood there with a heaving chest. After I had explained that I was just sleeping and apologized for not being more careful, he relaxed. He warned me not to do it again before he left.

The weekend was spent in bed with one of the guys periodically coming upstairs to check on me. By Monday, I was ready to be outside. Holly convinced me to take Monday off of school as well, which left me home alone again. I woke up late with a cough. I took a long hot shower hoping it would help. Which it did a little.

"Maybe we should take a breathing treatment before anyone stops by and freaks out." Cora suggested as I coughed again.

I pulled the machine out from under my bathroom sink and sat on the floor for the twenty minutes it took to do the treatment. When I was done, I cleaned the machine and put it away before heading downstairs. My stomach growled, so I made a quick peanut butter and jelly sandwich before plopping down on the couch to do homework. The breathing treatment made me jittery, and my hands were shaking, making it hard to write.

I heard the key turn in the lock just before the front door opened. Easton quickly ran up the stairs before I had a chance to say anything. A moment later he came back down with a frantic look on his face. He glanced in my direction as he ran for the door while pulling out his phone. He skidded to a stop and slowly put his phone back in his pocket before saying anything.

"You aren't in bed." He accused.

"I am feeling much better. And I don't have to be in bed all the time." I told him as I tried to write something on my paper. My hand was shaking so bad that I could hardly read my own handwriting. I sighed and put my books on the coffee table.

"Why are you shaking like that?" he asked as he walked over to the couch and sat down. He grabbed my hand as he studied it.

"Easton, it's fine. It will pass in about an hour." I smiled before reaching for my sandwich. Easton grabbed it first and took a bite. "Hey. That's mine." I said as I snatched it from his hand.

"I seem to recall you doing the same thing to me not long ago." He chuckled. "Plus, this is my lunch break. I won't have time to eat by the time I get back to the school."

"You guys are ridiculous, you know that?" I said as I stood. I heard Easton's footsteps as he followed me into the kitchen. I pulled out the lunch meat, cheese, lettuce, and a tomato and set them on the counter. "I am fine. I don't need you all checking in on me constantly." I pulled out two pieces of bread and started to make a sandwich. A coughing fit had me stepping back from the counter. When it was done, I pressed a hand to my stomach with a groan.

"Yeah, you are clearly fine." Easton said sarcastically as he put his arms around me. I leaned against him and closed my eyes. Why was he so comfortable to be with? "At least your fever is gone. Now, what can I do to help with this cough and shaking?"

"The cough will pass eventually. The shaking is a side effect of my breathing treatment and will go away in a little bit." That was the wrong thing to say. Easton tensed as he looked down at me.

"Breathing treatment?" He said as he gave me an unreadable expression. "As in, you can't breathe?"

"As in, a medicine that helps open my airways. Coughing causes muscle spasms that can make your airways tighter. Opening them makes it so I cough less." I pushed off his chest and took a step back. "I can breathe just fine." He grumbled something I couldn't understand as I finished making his sandwich. I turned back around to face him and handed him his food. "Now, eat up before you have to go back to work."

We settled back on the couch and Easton ate quietly. I started coughing again. Easton put his arm around me and pulled me close to his side. When the coughing stopped, I sagged against him. I looked up at him and our eyes met. He studied my face slowly before he tucked a few strands of hair behind my ear. His gaze lowered to my lips for several seconds before returning to my eyes.

"Please, don't pull away." Cora begged. *"Just live in the moment for once and not overthink everything."*

Easton's head slowly lowered, giving me plenty of time to pull away. I was still debating if I wanted to pull away or not when his lips pressed softly to mine, and my mind was made up. I wanted him to kiss me. I returned his kiss, which seemed to be encouragement enough for him to tangle his hand in my hair and deepen the kiss. We sat there kissing until his phone rang, snapping me back to reality.

I pulled back and blinked several times. What had I done? I had made a promise to not get involved with anyone but my mate, and I had just kissed Easton. I looked into his eyes, which were a dark green instead of his normal bright color. I slowly sat back as my head cleared. I watched as his eyes slowly lightened back to their normal color. He took in my expression and an almost panicked look entered his eyes.

"Carr, I'm…" He started to say but stopped when I shook my head.

"No, it's okay, Easton." I ran my hand through my hair as I stood. Oh man, what had I done. "That shouldn't have happened." I whispered as I headed for the stairs.

"Carly, wait." He followed me up to my room but stopped before entering. "Please, can we talk about this?" He pleaded.

"That was…" Cora breathed out. Then she seemed to come to her senses. *"Oh no! Our mate. What did we do?"*

"Yeah, what did we do?" I asked her. I closed my eyes briefly before turning to look back at Easton. He watched me as if waiting for me to blow up and start yelling. "East, we shouldn't have…I can't…I made a promise." I finally said.

"A promise? To who?" he asked in a stiff voice and his eyes darkened slightly.

"Yes, a promise, Easton." I said in exasperation. I felt a tear slip onto my cheek. "Cora and I promised to never get involved with anyone but our mate." I ran my hand through my hair again in agitation. "That should never have happened." I said again softly.

Easton's eyes turned almost black for a split second before clearing again. He took slow steps as he approached me, all the while studying me.

"I'm sorry, Carly." He reached up and gently wiped the tear off my cheek. "I should never have pushed you, and I'm sorry for that." His phone rang again, and he sighed. "I need to get back to the school, are you going to be okay?" he asked wiping the last of my tears away.

"I'm sorry, Easton." I said again dropping my gaze to the floor. I don't know why I felt like I was letting him down.

He hooked his finger under my chin and lifted my face up to his. "There is nothing for you to be sorry about, Carly. I am the one who is sorry for pushing you."

"You're sorry for pushing me into the kiss, but not the kiss itself?" I asked confused. As far as apologies went, it was terrible. But in all honesty, I wasn't really sorry for the kiss either. I was only sorry that I felt so guilty for enjoying it so much.

His dimple appeared as he smiled at me. His eyes darkened a little again. "Yeah, I'm going to have to say I'm sorry for not being sorry for the actual kiss." He leaned forward and kissed my forehead before stepping back. At my bedroom door he paused and looked back at me. "Max will be here in a few hours to hang out until mom comes over. Thanks for a great lunch break, Carly." He said with a wink and then he was gone.

I stared after him. *"What the heck was that? He kissed us again after we told him we could not get involved with him."* Cora huffed. *"If you didn't have a cough, I would suggest we go for a run. I don't even know if I want to see him again."*

"Says the one who begged me to allow the kiss to happen." I scoffed at her.

"I don't know what came over me. He must have some magic voodoo powers or something." Cora sulked.

I shook my head and climbed back into bed. *"That kiss was..."* I sighed. That kiss had been sweet and tender. He had made me feel like he cared for me, like I was the most important thing to him. *"His eyes going dark like that, was that his wolf?"* I asked curiously.

"I believe so." Cora said thoughtfully. *"I'm surprised his wolf let him kiss us, considering he is able to find his mate."*

"Maybe his wolf is frustrated that he hasn't found his mate yet, and needed a little kiss to get him through until he finds her." I said with a shrug. The very thought of Easton kissing another had my stomach knotting.

I groaned at my own foolishness. I got up and stomped to my closet. I needed a little fresh air. I pulled on some warm clothes, a beanie and my tennis shoes and headed downstairs. I sent a quick text to Jason to let him know that I was going for a quick walk to get some fresh air, that I was taking the small loop around the residency district, and that I would let him know when I returned.

The day was a little chilly and the autumn leaves were colorful. The wind blew, causing several of the dying leaves to blow off the trees and flutter around before settling on the ground. Birds sang as they flew from tree to tree. All-in-all, it was a peaceful day. I walked slowly as I took in the beauty around me. I began to play with the bracelet on my wrist. I looked down at it and sighed. This witch's bracelet masked my scent, but if Dax was a tracker and already knew where I was, did I really need to keep it on.

I returned home after only ten minutes and sent Jason a text. I went back to the living room and started on my homework again. Now that the jitters were gone, writing was so much easier. I was surprised when Max walked in, and I quickly looked at the time. Sure enough, several hours had gone by. I was feeling much more rejuvenated after getting some fresh air and sunshine.

"What do you want for dinner?" I asked as I put my books down.

"I can make something if you are hungry." Max said as he sat in a chair. "Easton said you are coughing now."

"Easton can just take a chill pill. I'm fine. I get coughs sometimes. They can last from a few days to a few weeks." I headed for the kitchen. "The sooner you boys accept that this is normal for me, the sooner we can all get back to a normal life." I looked in the fridge. I needed to get more food. "I hope you aren't too comfortable." I called as I headed for the front door. "We are headed out."

"No. We are staying here." Max said, coming to his feet. "Your Papa Bear gave me strict orders to keep you here."

I pulled out my phone and sent Jason a text telling him Max and I were going to the store. I again promised to let him know when we got back. A second later I got a text telling me to be careful and to not overdue it. I smirked as I handed my phone to Max. "Ready?" I asked. He shook his head in disbelief as he handed me my phone and we left.

*   *   *

It was like shopping with a toddler. Max put in so much junk food it was a wonder how he stayed in such good shape. I kept putting things back and he would complain. He made disgusted faces as I put in vegetables and other healthier foods. He sulked all the way back to the house about not getting anything good and how he was going to starve.

"Are you always like this?" I finally asked.

"Like what?" Max asked as he sat at the kitchen table and watched me put the groceries away.

I looked at him with a hand on my hip. "Like a baby. Seriously Max, you are acting like a pouty child." My scolding ended in a coughing fit, and Max was at my side instantly with a worried expression.

I brushed off his concern and continued putting things away. I spent the next couple hours cooking dinner and baking brownies with fudge frosting. Max watched me the whole time, and by the time I set a plate in front of him, he was practically drooling. His eyes rolled back in his head as he took his first bite of the green beans.

"So, if you don't find your mate within the first few days after your shift, can I apply for the job?" Max asked as he shoveled more food into his mouth.

I was laughing so hard that I ended up in a coughing fit. When I regained control, I wiped tears from my eyes and saw Jason, Easton, and Holly walking through the doorway. The memory of our kiss flashed in my mind when I saw Easton. I avoided meeting his eyes as I fought the blush that wanted to surface.

"What did we miss that was so funny you almost died laughing?" Jason asked with a smile.

I stood and moved back to the counter to dish up food for everyone. I was still smiling as I put plates on the table. "Max here was asking for an application." He winked at me as he took another bite.

"An application for what?" Holly asked as she sat down and took a bite. "Wow, this is amazing! Where did you learn to cook?"

"I just combine what sounds good." I shrugged and took a bite. "Max wanted to stake a possible claim in case I don't find my mate within a few days of turning eighteen."

Jason smacked the back of Max's head, but moaned when he took a bite of his food. I snuck a glance at Easton, he was glaring at Max. He slowly took a bite and chewed. His eyes snapped to me. "This is really good." He took another bite. "Why have we been eating Max's barely edible food when you could have been cooking?"

"Because my cub has been sick, and she didn't need to be cooking for you boys while not feeling well." Jason shot Easton a glare.

Holly laughed. "Papa Bear is right. And your son was only teasing, sweetheart." Holly patted Jason's hand. I smirked at Easton, and he glared at me, but his dimple was showing, so it wasn't very threatening.

After dinner was done, I started cleaning up, but kept coughing. Holly shooed me out and she took over. I sat on the couch, reading a book for English while half listening to Jason, Max, and Easton talk about their assignments as instructors and Jason's latest duties.

"Don't worry about a substitute, your mother will take the sparring class and I will be taking over strategy for the next couple of days." Jason was saying, and I glanced over at him. I must have missed something. "You and Max will need to leave first thing in the morning if you are to be back by Thursday.

I looked over at Easton and felt like someone was ripping a part of me away. What was happening to me? Cora began whining and pacing restlessly. I dropped my gaze to my lap and concentrated on breathing normally. Why would it bother me to have Easton leave for a few days? I was so confused.

"Are you feeling okay, Carly?" Max's question broke into my thoughts and my head snapped up. "You don't look like you are feeling very well. You lost your color."

I blinked and then nodded. "I'm fine." I said quietly.

Easton put an arm along the back of the couch and leaned close. Warmth spread through me at his closeness. "Liar." He whispered against my ear. I closed my eyes and shook my head. I fought against the urge to lean against him.

"You do look a bit pale." Jason commented. "Easton, why don't you take Carly up to her room and then we need to head out." He turned his attention to Max, and they started to talk about what Max's class had been working on.

Easton helped me to my feet before following me upstairs. I had my arms wrapped around myself, trying to calm down. Easton grabbed my arm and stopped me before I entered my room. "What's the matter, Carly?" he asked as he looked at my face.

"I don't know." I whispered, refusing to look in his eyes. Easton put his arms around me, and I wrapped my arms around his neck, returning his hug.

Easton's embrace was warm and comforting. I buried my face into his chest as I squeezed my eyes shut. I didn't want him to go. One of his hands moved from my back, and I felt my phone slide out of my back pocket.

"What's your unlock code?" He asked.

"Did you just take my phone out of my pocket?" My voice was muffled by his shirt.

"Your code, Carr." He said again. I told him my code and a few minutes later my phone slid back into my pocket. "I programmed mine and Max's numbers into your phone. If you need anything while we are gone, call or text us."

I didn't say anything. Easton's arms tightened around me, and my feet were lifted off the ground as he took two steps forward. He set my feet back on the ground once we were in my room. "You could have said to back up." I said as I shook my head.

He leaned back so he could see my face, and my hands slid down his chest. The corner of his mouth was curved up slightly. "You didn't seem like you wanted to move." I let out a slow breath and looked down. "What's going on, Carr?" Easton's voice was soft, and I couldn't help the pull to look into his eyes.

"I don't know." I said again. "I just don't know." I tried to step away, but he didn't let me go. "Easton, we shouldn't." I whispered.

"I know you made that promise, but I think you should make me the exception." Easton's eyes twinkled as he spoke.

"Why is that?" I asked suspiciously as I studied his face. His eyes darkened slightly.

"For starters, we spent a good twenty minutes earlier making out." I felt my cheeks heat.

"No way it was twenty minutes." I argued. It couldn't have been that long. Easton's smile grew.

"You made me a sandwich, then we kissed until I had to go back to work. So, I guess you are right, it was quite a bit longer." I didn't think my cheeks could get any redder and Easton chuckled.

He slowly lowered his head while watching me closely. I knew I should stop him, but I didn't want to. When our lips met, I melted. My arms went around his neck and pulled him closer. This kiss was different. Last time it had been slow and sweet, this time was filled with longing and need. Easton pulled away enough to start kissing along my neck.

When he kissed the spot where mates mark each other, a shiver ran down my spine and I felt him smile against my skin. He moved back up until he reached the sensitive spot just below my ear. I stifled a moan when he concentrated his attention there. After a few seconds he returned his lips to mine.

His hand moved to the back of my neck as he deepened the kiss. I pressed myself closer to him, needing to feel his warmth and comfort. I did not want him to go.

"Easton, are you ready to go?" Jason called from downstairs a while later.

We were both breathing hard as Easton slowly pulled away. He rested his forehead against mine until our breathing returned to normal. "I have to go." He whispered before pressing a kiss to my forehead. "I'll text you in the morning to see how you are doing." He stole one more kiss and left. I heard him talking to his dad about travel plans as they left the house.

"*Why can't I think rationally when he is around?*" I asked Cora as I sank onto the edge of my bed. My lips still tingled from his kiss.

"*The real question is why* does *he* continue *to want to kiss us when he knows he doesn't have a chance, since we are waiting for our mate?*" Cora questioned back. "*The chances of finding one's mate in one's pack is rare. He knows that.*"

I ran a hand through my hair. Sighing, I put my face in my hands. What had changed between Easton and I to make me miss him when we weren't together, well more than I usually did before the summer? How did he make me feel better with just a look or a touch? Obviously, we had kissed, but these confusing feelings were happening before today.

If I were to be honest with myself, I had always found Easton cute and I was drawn to him. Maybe that is why his constant teasing had affected me so much. Now that he wasn't going out of his way to tease me, I was seeing a different side of him. One that was kind, protective and comforting.

Shaking my head, I tried to make sense of all the conflicting emotions I was feeling. I had been beyond upset to realize he was leaving for a few days. Just a simple hug from him had calmed my rising anxiety, and then that kiss. Why had I not stopped it? Why had I wanted him to kiss me, again?

"*Carly, I think you might* be *falling for Easton.*" Cora said softly.

"*I can't be falling in love with Easton.*" I protested. "*We promised not to get involved with anyone but our mate. I can't be in love with him.*" But even as I said it, I knew that it was true. I was falling hard for Easton Shepherd despite doing my best to guard myself from everyone. *"What are we going to do now?"* I groaned as I pulled my knees to my chest.

"*I think we should distance ourselves from him. Whenever we are with him, we can't help falling* even *more for him."* Cora said reluctantly.

A piece of my heart felt like it was breaking as the prospect of not having Easton with me started to settle in. Avoiding him used to be easy, now it felt wrong, but I had to do it. I would be eighteen in just two days and then I would find my mate. The sooner I found my mate, the sooner I could get over Easton.

Chapter 11

I sat in the back of my English class as the teacher talked about the book they were reading. Because of my accelerated pace, I was almost done with it while the class was barely halfway. Depression had taken over my brain, making it hard to concentrate on anything. I didn't even try to pay attention. I technically didn't even need this class to graduate.

Easton had messaged me first thing this morning asking how I was doing. I told him I was fine, and he called me a liar. He tried to get me to respond with more details, but I stopped replying.

My phone vibrated in my pocket, and I peeked at it to see who had messaged me. The text was from Jason asking if I was okay. I rolled my eyes and responded with a 'yes'. We messaged back and forth a few more times before I told him I had to go. Easton probably talked to his dad.

"Miss Brooks?" Mrs. Langley, the teacher, called. I looked up at her and she motioned me forward. I stood slowly and made my way up to her. Was I going to get in trouble for texting in class? "Collect your things, Mr. Morris is waiting for you in his office." She whispered.

Mr. Morris? Why would the principal be waiting for me? "Am I in trouble?" I asked anxiously.

"Oh no. He just has some things to discuss with you about your graduation requirements." Mrs. Langley smiled reassuringly.

I grabbed my backpack and headed for the principal's office. Even though Mrs. Langley had tried to reassure me that nothing was wrong, my anxiety was causing my heart to beat erratically.

I knocked on the thick, polished wood door of Mr. Morris's office and waited with my stomach in knots. He called for me to enter and I took a deep breath before I slowly turned the knob. I stepped inside before looking up. I paused in the doorway when I saw Mr. Morris sitting behind his desk with Alpha Callum standing next to him.

"You asked to see me?" I asked softly.

"Yes, please take a seat. We are just waiting on one more person." Mr. Morris said, gesturing to the chairs in front of the desk. Moving to a seat quickly, I sat on the edge of it and ran my hands over my jeans nervously. There was a quick knock on the door before Gamma Jason entered and took the chair next to me.

"Gamma Jason." Mr. Morris greeted. "You are the temporary guardian of Miss Brooks while her mother is away?"

"I am." Jason said, and I turned to look at him in surprise. Mom had only mentioned that she asked Jason and Holly to check in on me, not that they were my temporary guardians. He smiled in my direction. It wasn't his normal smile, and I got the feeling he was upset about something but trying to hide it from me. "What is this all about? Alpha, I didn't expect to see you here." A look passed between Jason and Alpha Callum that caused me to be on guard. Cora, too, felt like something wasn't right.

"There are a few things that we need to discuss." Alpha Callum answered. "But I think we should start with Mr. Morris's news." The way Alpha Callum was acting added to my unease.

I looked at Mr. Morris as he began talking. "I was reviewing your grades and classes to make sure you are still on track to graduate in nine weeks."

"Nine weeks? The school year is only half over." Jason said surprised.

"Yes. Miss Brooks has been on an accelerated track since Junior High in order to graduate early." Mr. Morris explained quickly. "Miss Brooks, you were only required to take Biology III and Sparring in order to graduate. Alpha Callum informed me that you passed all the required skills to graduate from Sparring immediately." I knew that. Alpha Callum said I would be done with sparring if I fought Jet. "Mr. Larson made a mistake when he gave you your midterm exam."

"What do you mean?" I asked, confused. The test had taken twice as long as expected and there were some questions on there that I didn't remember going over in class. I was ahead in my reading though and overall, the test hadn't been crazy difficult.

"Mr. Larson realized he had given you both the midterm and the final exams while he was grading your test." Mr. Morris eyed me for a few moments. "You passed both with a ninety-three percent."

"What does that mean?" Jason asked Mr. Morris, but his eyes were on me.

Mr. Morris crossed his arms over his chest and leaned back in his chair. "It means that Miss Brooks has completed all the requirements to graduate." He turned to me. "Congratulations, Carly. You are done." He gave me a big smile as I sat there, shocked. "You are still welcome to participate in the graduation ceremony at the end of the school year, but you are officially a graduate as of twenty minutes ago."

Jason laughed as he stood. He pulled me up and gave me a fatherly embrace. I was still dumbfounded. *"Wahoo!"* Cora cheered. *"Now, the whole 'no making out with a teacher rule' doesn't apply."*

"We are keeping our distance." I reminded her. *"You were the one to suggest it."*

"Now, I will let you have use of my office for whatever you need to, Alpha." Mr. Morris stood from his chair and left without another word.

Tension filled the room and Jason's hold on me tightened. Something was terribly wrong. I pushed away from him as I looked from him to Alpha Callum.

"What is it? What's wrong?" I asked as I wrapped my arms around myself, my chest already feeling tight. Was this why Jason started texting me?

"Carly, please sit down." Alpha's voice was soft while his expression remained blank.

"No." I said, shaking my head. "Just tell me."

"Carr, there was an attack early this morning." Jason lightly touched my elbow as Alpha Callum explained. "Beta Harry and Beta Sara were injured, but your mother was captured."

My breathing became ragged. Mom captured? Why would mom be captured? I looked up into Jason's face as I felt the sting of tears. My chin trembled and I shook my head. I bolted from the room. I didn't stop until I got to the packhouse. I was trembling so hard it took me a couple of tries to punch in the code to the side door correctly. Not bothering to change my clothes, I stepped onto the treadmill and ran.

I didn't bother wiping the tears off my face as I sprinted. I was gasping for air and coughing when a hand pushed the stop button. I slowed with the machine, not bothering to see who was there until I came to a complete stop.

Mike stood there with a pained expression. Both Mike's parents had been injured in the attack. "I'm so sorry." I choked out.

Mike pulled me into a hug, and I couldn't hold back my sobs anymore. He held me tight and allowed me to cry. When my tears finally stopped, Mike helped wipe my tears away.

"Your phone has been going off nonstop for about an hour." He sounded calm and not at all upset.

I sniffled and stepped back. "I'm sorry about your parents and about my breakdown." I said looking at the floor.

"My parents will be fine. Just a few scratches and bruises. They are on their way back right now." He shrugged. "And what are big brothers for if not to let their little sisters cry on their shoulder?"

I laughed. "Big brother? Little sister?" I sat down on the floor with my back against the wall.

"Of course. I know for a fact that Max and I feel very much like you are our sister." Mike sat down next to me and bumped my shoulder with his.

"You guys teased me mercilessly since the day mom and I became members of the pack." I said, confused.

"Did you ever wonder why we were the only ones to tease you?" he asked with a chuckle. "I thought Easton was going to get kicked out of school for fighting when he heard some boy talking about how cute you were. After the kid came back to school, he told everyone to leave you alone, otherwise the Triad would beat them up."

"That's why Easton got in the fight with Benson?" I asked in disbelief. "If you three were so protective of me, why did you tease me so much?"

"Brothers can tease their sisters, but no one else can. Plus, you were the only person to not cower or submit to us. It became a game of sorts to see who could get you to crack first. We may have gone overboard with it." He paused for a moment. "I am sorry for teasing you so much. I didn't realize that you took it so hard." I shrugged. It was all in the past and so much has happened since then. "Easton was so protective of you. I remember him giving me a black eye when we were sixteen because I took your jacket during a winter storm, and you didn't come back to school for a few weeks."

I laughed. I couldn't believe what I was hearing. This totally put a different spin on how I thought of them and their teasing. Mom had told me to not take it personally, but I did. Mom. "Do you know anything about the attack or who took my mom?" I asked softly.

His arm came around me as he gave me a side hug. I rested my head on his shoulder. "Sorry Carr, I don't know much. All I know is that the attack seemed odd. Dad told Alpha that the attackers seemed interested in your mom more than the others. No one was seriously injured. As suddenly as the attack started, it stopped. Your mom was the only one unaccounted for." I pulled my knees to my chest. My phone started to ring, but I ignored it. "It's Easton, want me to answer it for you?" I shook my head, and he handed it to me.

I accepted the phone and silenced the call. It rang again. I once again ignored the call before turning my phone off as I fought back the tears that wanted to fall. I wanted Easton. I wished he were the one here with me, and because of that, I needed to not take his calls. We sat quietly for a long while. Mike's phone rang and he answered it.

"Hel…Wow, chill man." Mike said. I could hear an angry male voice on the other end of the call and knew it was Easton. "No, she's fine." He sighed. "Carly just needs some time to process everything. Dude, you and Max need to not worry so much. I promise, she is safe." He chuckled. "I know because she is right here laying on me." I sat up and elbowed him in the stomach. "Oof. What was that for, Carr?"

"I am not laying on you. We are sitting next to each other." I got to my feet. "Now, I am leaving. Alone." I emphasized. "I need some time to myself."

"Hold up. I will walk you home and then you can have your alone time." Mike stood and started following me. "No man. She is handling the news of her mom remarkably well. I will call you later." Silence fell between us as we headed for my house.

Mike didn't come inside but reminded me to lock the door. I rolled my eyes but did as he said. I went to my room and sat on my bed to think. Mom was gone, targeted from what it sounded like. But, why? Had someone from the North Wind Pack seen her while she was out with the Betas? Was I in danger?

"Cora, what do make of all this?" I asked as I gathered a change of clean clothes. I was feeling a little agitated and it was making it harder to think.

"I think the North Wind Pack was involved. Your mom is an Omega. There is no reason to target her unless they were from North Wind." Cora agreed.

I headed for the bathroom. I needed a shower. *"Tomorrow we can meet with Alpha* Callum *and tell him about us hiding from the North Wind Pack. Maybe he will know how to get mom back."*

By the time I was showered and dressed, I felt like a caged animal. I had so much pent-up energy but couldn't seem to get rid of it. I tried running on my treadmill and pacing, then eating, but nothing seemed to calm my rising agitation. Cora, too, was restless. I took a second shower to rinse off the sweat from my second run. As I was pulling my hair into a ponytail, I noticed something on my neck. Leaning closer I turned slightly to get a better look.

"I can't believe he did that." Cora seethed. My own anger flared to life.

I ran to my room and grabbed my phone. I paced as I waited for it to turn back on from earlier. I can't believe I hadn't seen it until now. Granted I really hadn't showered and did the bare minimum to look presentable for school since Easton left. As soon as it was on, I clicked Easton's number. It rang four times before it was answered.

"Hey Carly. What's up?" Max's voice sounded cheerful, which only irritated me more.

"I need to talk with Easton." I said through clenched teeth. I had no idea why I was so mad, but I was.

"He's in the shower. I'm sure if you want to wait a few minutes he will be done soon."

"Get him on the phone, now, Max." I ordered.

"Okay, hold on." I wiped my brow while I listened to someone knock on a door and a muffled response. "Carly's on the phone." A pause. "I think you better take it now, East. She sounds pissed."

There was something moving in the background that I couldn't make out, but then Easton came on the line. "Hey, Carly."

"What have you done, Easton?" I growled as I pulled my sweatshirt off. I was getting a little too warm.

"Uh. I'm not exactly sure what you are referring to." Easton slowly responded. I could hear wariness in his voice.

I paced my room a few more times trying to cool my rising anger. This wasn't like me to get so fired up, but I was ready to kill him. "You gave me a hickey!" I yelled.

There was silence on the other end of the phone for a few minutes. "I did?" Easton sounded proud of himself. "Where is it?"

"Easton Shepherd, this is not a joking matter!" I snapped.

"Calm down, Carr." He chuckled. "It'll be okay, its only temporary."

"Don't tell me to calm down, because it's not okay!" I roared. "Nothing is okay. My mom has been taken, I feel out of control, and I am so freaking hot!" I took off my long-sleeved shirt and threw it on the ground in a huff.

"What do you mean you feel out of control and hot?" Easton asked, sounding serious.

"That's not the point, Easton!" I yelled. My breathing was coming fast, and I swiped my forehead again with a shaky hand. I stopped my pacing and looked at my trembling hand, then to the clock. It was a couple of hours until midnight. "I've got to go." I said quickly.

"Carly, wait!" East called out, but I hung up.

"Cora, I think we are shifting." I said as I moved to my window to make sure it was locked.

Cora was still restless, but agreed we needed to get to the basement. I ran from room to room locking windows and drawing the curtains closed. The pain began by the time I made it into the basement and locked the door. I turned on the generator so I could have some light and several fans going. I paced the small space, not sure what to do. The pain increased as the time ticked by.

I felt like I was burning alive while every bone in my body was breaking. The pain was so intense that I was laying on one of the cots while tossing and turning. Cora tried to speak encouraging words to me but stopped a while ago when the pain had us both crying out. Another wave hit me, and I screamed as I curled into a ball.

"The bracelet!" Cora cried. *"We need to take off the bracelet."*

With a trembling hand, I unclasped the bracelet on my wrist and watched it slide to the floor. The pain immediately intensified, and I began to sob. I tried to relax and not fight it, but it was hard. "I don't think I can do this." I told Cora. "I'm not strong enough."

"Let me take control, Carly. Let me help us get through this." Cora soothed.

I closed my eyes and tried to picture Cora. What would she look like? Out of the blackness of my mind, a grey wolf with dark blue eyes emerged walking towards me.

The wolf smiled and wagged her tail. She had one darker ear that gave her a playful look, but she also radiated power and strength. Cora. She gave me a nod as another wave of pain hit. This one was worse than any others. I felt my consciousness slipping and then the wolf was gone, swallowed up in the blackness.

I yawned and stretched as I woke up. Groaning, I got to my feet slowly. I felt different. Opening my eyes I saw that I was much lower to the ground than normal. Confused, I looked around. I was still in the bunker, but everything looked different. The colors were sharper, and I could see more detail.

"Morning, Carly." Cora beamed.

"Good morning to you, too." I laughed at her cheerfulness. *"What happened last night? Why do I feel so weird?"*

Cora chuckled. *"You feel weird because you are a wolf still."*

"A wolf?" I looked down and saw two furry grey legs and large paws. *"We shifted!"* I yelled in excitement.

"We did." Cora chuckled. *"But it is time to shift back. You ready?"*

I nodded and closed my eyes. I envisioned myself as a human and I began to feel my bones rearranging. Thankfully, this time wasn't painful, just uncomfortable. Once I shifted back, Cora told me she was going to take a nap and I smiled. I had shifted. I moved towards the door, but I kicked something small as I walked by the cot.

I looked down and saw my bracelet. I slowly bent down and picked it up. I put it back on before unlocking the door. I prayed that since I was a full wolf now, the bracelet's magic wouldn't make me weak anymore.

When I got up to the main level, I noticed it was still really early. The sun was just starting to rise, barely lighting the sky. I felt so much stronger and full of energy.

I jogged upstairs and was getting dressed for the day when I saw my phone on the floor. I picked it up and saw I had seventeen missed calls between Easton, Max, and Mike. I sighed as I sat on the bed and dialed Easton's number. It only rang twice.

"Carly! Thank heavens. Are you okay?" Easton sounded panicked.

"Calm down, Easton. I'm fine." I chuckled. I couldn't help it. I was in a really good mood. "I just wanted to call and say sorry for last night. I was just overwhelmed with all the news that was heaped on me."

There was a pause before Easton spoke again. "It's okay, Carr. What other news did you get?"

"As of yesterday, I am a High School graduate." I told him with a smile. That fact was finally sinking in, and I was ecstatic.

"Wait, what?" Easton sounded confused. "The school year isn't even half over."

"I have been taking accelerated classes during the school year and extra classes during the summer for six years so I could graduate early. Mr. Larson accidentally gave me the final as well as the midterm, and I passed both. And my match with Jet allowed me to pass the Sparring curriculum. Mr. Morris let me know yesterday, right before Alpha and Papa Bear told me about my mom." I laid back on my bed and stared at my ceiling.

"That's amazing, Carr. Congratulations on graduating." He hesitated and cleared his throat. "What happened last night? I have never heard you sound so angry before. And you said you felt out of control and hot."

I wanted to tell him. I was so excited that I had finally shifted. I felt amazing and my cough seemed to be gone. But I couldn't. Not yet. Not while mom was missing. "I think I was just a little stressed after hearing about mom. I feel so alone without her here. East, I'm worried." I settled for a half-truth.

"I know." His voice softened. "We have a meeting in an hour, but we should be back by dinner. Dad said to meet at your house so we can go over what we know about your mom's disappearance and what the plan is to find her."

"Thank you, Easton." I said with a smile. "I will see you tonight then."

"When I get back, we can celebrate your graduation." There was a flirtatious note to his voice.

I felt my cheeks heat. "Why do I get the feeling that you are talking about kissing me again?"

Easton's chuckle caused butterflies to take flight in my stomach. "Baby, kissing you is always on my mind. But I was thinking more along the lines of a movie or something, since the guys will be there too."

"Hmm, I might be okay with that, as long as it's an action movie." I said with a smile.

"A girl after my own heart." Easton laughed. "I'll send you a text when we are out of the meeting and heading home. See you tonight, Carr."

We hung up and I sighed. Then I groaned. A movie night was not keeping my distance. Now that I had shifted, I would be able to sense my mate. I needed to cut Easton out of the equation because the chances of finding your mate within your own pack was rare. And the more in love I fell with Easton, the harder it would be to want to find my mate. When he got back, I was going to tell him that I couldn't see him anymore.

Chapter 12

I jumped in the shower and got dressed in a cap sleeved shirt that fit me perfectly. I hadn't worn it before because I had stuck with long sleeves and large hoodies. It was weird not feeling cold, but I liked that I could wear some of my cuter clothes. I was putting on my makeup when I caught sight of the hickey again. I lightly touched it as a smile spread on my lips.

The memory of that kiss resurfaced, and I sighed. It had been earth shattering. Then I remembered seeing Easton with Marissa in the hall at school and I growled. Who did she think she was, touching Easton? And why was Easton touching her?

I ran my hand through my newly curled hair in agitation. The thought of him with another woman made me want to punch something. He wasn't mine to be getting possessive over. I reminded myself. He wasn't mine. I roughly pulled on a pair of tennis shoes before heading outside. I needed a distraction from Easton, and I needed to meet with Alpha this morning to talk about the attack on my mom.

I walked slowly, admiring the clear blue sky and autumn leaves. A cool breeze blew, but I barely felt it and I smiled. This was going to be an adjustment, but I was excited for this change.

I got to the place on the path to the packhouse where there were a lot of thick trees. A sense of unease caused the hair on the back of my neck to rise. Cora woke and began sniffing the air.

"We should head back home. Something isn't right." she said anxiously.

I turned around and froze. Dax stood on the path behind me with a predatory grin. "I see you managed to shake your guard dogs." He laughed.

"What do you want, Dax?" I asked, annoyed that he was dampening my good mood.

"We are surrounded." Cora cautioned me. *"It's weird, they don't have a scent, but I can hear them."*

"I want my mate to come spend time with me." His grin turned wicked. "What do you say? Are we going to do this the easy way or the hard way?"

"He's definitely not our mate." Cora's hackles rose as she growled.

"We both know that you are not my mate. What do you want from me?" I snapped. I kept my eyes glued to him. I didn't trust him. There was something about this guy that set off warning bells, and I knew I needed to get away.

Dax clicked his tongue. He lifted his hand and a silver chain dangled between his fingers. He tossed it to me, and I caught it. I looked at it and gasped when I recognized my mother's bracelet. He chuckled at my response. "I want you to come with me before I lose my patience."

I clenched my fist around the bracelet as I fought back tears. Dax had taken my mom. I felt someone move behind me and I bolted down the path, dodging Dax's attempt to grab me. I ran as fast as I could back home and locked the door behind me. I pulled out my phone and called Jason as I ran upstairs.

"Come on. Come on." I muttered anxiously as I listened to it ring. It went to voicemail. I tried calling Holly but got the same result. I was looking around desperately, trying to figure out what I could use to defend myself.

"Swap the bracelets, Carr." Cora told me. *"They are individualized, remember? Your mom's won't mask your scent, but it will look like you still have yours on. If they manage to take us, then the pack can track us."*

After I exchanged my bracelet, I pulled the first aid kit from the hall closet. It held all of our witch's creams and powders. "We need to make Dax and his men go nose blind, since my scent won't be masked." I grabbed a bag of red powder and ran downstairs.

The powder was supposed to be used in small amounts along your path to prevent whoever was tracking you to lose your scent. I didn't have the luxury to use small amounts. I dragged a chair to the front door and used it to hang the pouch over the entrance. I carefully tied floss to the pouch and tied the other end to the doorknob. Now, when the door opened, the pouch would dump on the person. The powder would do what it was designed to do and nose blind whoever inhaled it.

I ran to the kitchen and tried calling Jason again. He still didn't answer. *"Try Easton."* Cora suggested.

Someone banged on the front door. I clicked Easton's number and turned down the volume so no one would be able to hear his voice if he answered. If he did pick up the phone, then he would be able to hear what was going on.

I left my phone and my bracelet on the counter as I began rummaging through the cabinets, looking for something useful. The front door slammed open followed by several men coughing. I whirled around to see Dax, looking murderous, in the kitchen doorway. His face was contorted in rage.

"Did you really think you could escape me, little Carly?" He growled as he stomped up to me.

He slapped me so hard that I hit the counter and my arm slid across the top, sending my phone crashing to the floor with the extra bracelet. He grabbed my hair and yanked me close to him. I let out a cry of pain.

"You should have come easily. It pains me to have to damage that beautiful face of yours." He was shaking with anger.

"Where is my mom?" I asked through clenched teeth.

"Don't worry, Sweetheart. You and your so-called mom will be together again soon." Dax ran his nose along my jaw, and I shivered in disgust. He inhaled deeply then cursed. "That powder, what was it?" He yelled in my face.

"What powder?" I gritted out. He slapped me again and a cry of pain escaped my lips as I landed hard on the floor.

"Damian." Dax barked, and the man with the scar on his face handed Dax a cloth.

Dax approached me and I scooted back. He grabbed a fistful of my hair again and slammed the cloth over my mouth and nose. I tried to scream for help, but it was muffled. I struggled against Dax's hold. My vision began to fade, and Dax's smug smile was the last thing I saw.

Voices sounded from far away, rousing me from the darkness. I tried to open my eyes, but they felt heavy. I slowly sat up and looked around. I was in the backseat of a car, sitting between two large men. When they saw me moving around, the man to my right said something I couldn't quite make out.

Someone from the front seat handed back a syringe. I tried to shake my head and fight the man as he brought the needle close to me. The men all laughed as I lost the battle, and the syringe was stabbed into my leg. Blackness once again consumed me.

The cycle continued several more times. I would wake up only for them to stab me with a syringe. Each time I tried to fight them off and each time I lost.

This time when I woke, I was being dragged between two large men down a hall lined with doors. I tried to pull away from them, but my muscles felt like jelly. They ignored my weak attempts to get away and continued dragging me until we reached the far end of the hall. The man on my right unlocked a door and opened it. They dragged me in and dropped me on the floor before turning and walking out. I heard the lock slide into place.

I looked around to try to get my bearings. I took in the room I was being held prisoner in. It was a medium-sized bedroom, not much bigger than my room at home. There was a queen sized four poster bed in the middle of the wall, flanked by matching nightstands.

On the opposite wall there were two doors that were slightly ajar. I dragged myself to the closest one and finished pushing the door open the rest of the way. It was an empty closet. I moved to the next door and found a bathroom. I pulled myself inside before closing and locking the door.

"Cora, where are we? What's wrong with me? Why can't I move my legs?" I asked as I rubbed my legs, trying to bring strength back into them.

"I don't know. They kept us pretty drugged. I don't even know how much time has passed since they took us." Cora said angrily. She was frustrated with not knowing where we were.

I shook my head and fought the tears that threatened to fall. I continued to rub my legs as I tried to think of what to do. I sat there for a long time before I heard the bedroom door open, and I tensed.

"Where is she?" Dax asked angrily.

"She was right there when we left." A male voice said. "The bathroom door is closed, maybe she's in there."

A banging rocked the door at my back. "I'm busy! Go away!" I yelled.

"Open the door, Princess." Dax ordered. "I have someone who is desperate to see you."

The tone of his voice had me hesitating with my initial reaction to refuse. What if it was mom? I shakily got to my feet and slowly unlocked the door. As soon as I did, the door was pushed open and Dax grabbed my arm, dragging me back into the bedroom.

My legs gave out as Dax shoved me forward. I hit the ground hard, and he laughed. "Carly!" Mom cried and I looked up to see her struggling between the two guys that had brought me to the room.

"Let her go." Dax said in an amused voice.

Mom pulled free and ran to me. She wrapped her arms around me protectively. "What have you done to her?" Mom growled out.

"It will wear off soon enough. See what doing things the hard way gets you, Princess. We had to use more than we expected to keep you docile. You just kept putting up a fight." Dax smiled at me causing my skin to crawl. "I like a woman with fire in her. Maybe when the Alpha is done with you, I might be able to get some time with you before I head out." I glared at Dax as he waved at us dismissively. "You are awfully protective of a pup that isn't even yours." He commented as he and the others headed for the door. "Enjoy your evening together. Tomorrow will prove to be eventful." Dax gave me a smirk before closing the door.

Mom continued to hug me tight as we sat in the quiet. I clung to her as relief flooded me. She was alive and unharmed, well at least from what I could see. Together we could escape this place and go into hiding again. We would be okay. Then something Dax had said came back to me. I pulled back and looked at mom's face. "What did he mean when he said you were protective of a pup that wasn't yours?"

Tears filled mom's eyes as she looked at me. "I planned on telling you on your birthday." she said softly. I looked at her in surprise as I scooted away from her. "Carly, you don't understand. Please let me explain." She begged when she saw my hurt and confused expression.

"If you aren't my mom then who are you?" I asked angrily. Cora stood stiffly as she listened carefully.

"I am your guard, assigned to you by your father Alpha Kyle of the North Wind Pack." she said softly.

"Explain." I ground out. How could this woman claim to be my guard and pretend to be my mom yet never think to tell me who I was?

"Alpha Kyle attended an Alpha Conference hosted by the Alpha King. There he found his mate, Princess Brooke, the youngest child of the Alpha King. Their binding ceremony was held the second day of the conference and she returned to the North Wind Pack with Alpha Kyle. The pack was excited for such a powerful Luna. Only Alpha Kyle's brother, Kain, seemed unhappy with the union." I listened closely. Something about this story sounded strangely familiar. "A daughter was born within the first year of their marriage. Kain had disliked the little girl. He had done nothing to harm the child, but Luna Brooke became very protective of you."

"Me?" I breathed out.

Mom gave me a sad smile. "Yes, you are the daughter of Alpha Kyle and Luna Brooke. You were three when Luna Brooke found out that she was expecting a boy. Kain became enraged. Alpha Kyle assigned guards to watch over you and our Luna. I was to protect you at all costs. A few days after the announcement for the upcoming birth of the future Alpha, Kain rounded up followers and attacked the packhouse. Luna Brooke told me to take you and run. Both Alpha Kyle and Luna Brooke were killed in the attack. With the help of my grandmother, we were able to escape undetected. I took you to my sister's home in a nearby pack."

"Your grandmother? She was the witch." I said as some of the pieces from what I had thought were dreams, started falling into place. A fire. People screaming and running. The fear and confusion. A woman begging me to go and saying she loved me. A man with blue eyes telling me to be brave. A kind old lady.

Mom nodded before continuing. "We were there for only a few months when I heard about members from the North Wind Pack wanting to enter the pack lands. I didn't hesitate. I took you and escaped again. We were living as rogues, moving from place to place, trying to stay out of sight. We were on our own for a year when I found a waterfall with a large pool that it emptied into. You knew how to swim and knew not to go into the water without me. We were running low on supplies, so I left you hidden in a cave halfway up the rock behind the falls. When I got back, I nearly had a heart attack. You were playing with three boys and there was a couple sitting on a blanket not far away."

"I found out that one of the boys was the couple's son and the other two were their son's friends. They introduced themselves. Gamma Jason started asking questions. Where were we from? Did we have a place to go? Would we be willing to meet with their Alpha? You seemed so happy playing with kids your age, that I gave in. I met with Alpha Callum, and he accepted us into his pack. We have been in the Silver Moon Pack ever since." I stood and began to pace. The weakness in my legs was finally starting to go away.

"I am the daughter of Alpha Kyle and Luna Brooke." I said slowly. "What is my real name then?" I turned and looked at the woman I had thought of as my mother for the last fifteen years.

"Your real name is Carly Johnson. I told everyone our last name was Brooks in honor of your mother."

"Who are you?" I asked with a furrowed brow.

"My name is Savannah Trenton, one of the top guards of the North Wind Pack." Mom got to her feet and faced me. "I know I am not your real mother, and I could never hope to replace her, but Carly, I truly love you as if you were my own." Mom wiped at her tears.

"Why do they want me? I am no threat to them. They killed my parents and the heir, Alpha Kain has the pack. Why not just leave me alone?" I asked as fear started to fill me.

"They want to kill us." Cora said quietly.

"Kain and his mate had a son a few months before you were born. North Wind Pack law says that if a male heir is not available, the mate of the oldest daughter will be the new Alpha of the pack. Kain tried to convince Alpha Kyle to sign a contract that would bind you to his son as a chosen mate. Your parents were furious and told Kain that you would not be with anyone but your actual mate." Mom sighed as she sat on the edge of the bed. "Kain came to visit me in my cell. He wanted to find you before you found your mate. My guess is that he is still wanting you and his son to be together so that they can rightfully take over the pack without fear of the Alpha King stepping in."

"We will not be with anyone but our actual mate." Cora growled as she began to pace.

I wholeheartedly agreed. I knew that Dax was, for sure, not my mate now that Cora and I had shifted. "How long has it been since you were captured?" I asked. If mom knew how long she had been here, then I could know how long it had been since I was kidnapped.

"They attacked us nearly two weeks ago. But it took us three days to get here." She answered. That would mean I have been missing for almost two weeks. They kept me drugged for two weeks! Anger filled my veins, fueling my pacing. Cora snarled. She wanted to rip Dax apart. "You've shifted." Mom said with a small smile. "You don't seem so… human."

I smiled at her. "I switched my bracelet for yours at the house before they grabbed me, so that the pack could hopefully track my scent. Then I used the powder to cause Dax and a couple of his guys to go nose blind so they wouldn't be able to tell." Mom laughed and gave me a proud smile. "And I found out I completed all the requirements to graduate. So, I am officially done with high school."

Mom jumped to her feet and pulled me into a crushing hug. "I am so proud of you, sweetheart. When we get out of here, we need to celebrate."

Thoughts of a movie night and celebrating with Easton and the guys caused a pang of sadness. They probably panicked once they realized I wasn't home. Papa Bear was, more than likely, tearing apart the pack and neighboring packs looking for me.

I pushed thoughts of them from my mind. I needed to concentrate on the here and now. I needed to focus on surviving. "Any ideas on how to get out of here?" I asked, stepping back from mom, and looking around the room.

Chapter 13

Morning came quickly and we still hadn't thought of a plan to escape. The window had been cemented shut, and the door was locked. At this point, our only option was to wait and see what they wanted. As I laid on the bed, my mind replayed what mom had told me about my past.

Snatches of memory of playing with Easton, Mike and Max at the waterfall floated back to me. Easton had asked me if I was new to the pack, and I told him that I was only staying for a little while. He had grabbed my hand and told me that he didn't want me to go. He even offered to stay at the waterfall with me if I didn't want to be with the whole pack.

I replayed all my memories of Easton. Silent tears coursed down my cheeks. I missed him so much. Cora missed him too. Blasted Easton Shepherd. Why did I have to fall in love with him? I wiped the tears from my face and got up. There was no way I would be able to sleep. I walked around the room again, trying to figure out what I could use to get out of here.

Mom got out of the bed not long after I did. We were both restless. This waiting game was torture. I just wanted to know what was going to happen so I could plan for what was to come next.

The door finally opened and Dax stepped into the room. He grabbed my arm in a painful grip. One of his goons grabbed mom and we were both pulled down the hall. Now that I had a clear head, I took in my surroundings. If I had to guess, I would say we were in a packhouse. We were dragged down two large flights of stairs. I made note that our prison room was on the third floor. We went down another long hallway before I was shoved into a room halfway down.

I turned and glared at Dax. He smirked at me, and I punched him in the face as hard as I could. He staggered back a few steps, crashing against a bookcase. He shook his head, then gave me a shocked look before wiping blood from his nose. When he saw it, his expression hardened. He took an aggressive step towards me, but a deep male voice stopped him.

"That's enough, Dax." I turned to see a tall man with blue eyes and light brown hair sitting behind a desk. I hadn't even noticed him when I was shoved in the room. He studied me for a few moments before standing. "You look just like your mother, except you have your father's eyes." He said with a scowl.

"I want my payment." Dax said firmly. "Double because of how big of a pain she is."

The muscle worked in the man's jaw before he gave Dax a smile. "So be it." The door opened again, and six large men entered. Dax and his guys were large but compared to the newcomers, they were nothing. "Take Dax and his men to get their...payment." He instructed and soon all that remained in the room was this mystery man, two guards, mom, and me.

"Kain, it has been a long time since I saw you last." Mom sneered.

I looked at my mom and then back to Kain as he retook his seat behind the desk. He gestured for us to sit, but I glared at him. "No thanks. I would rather stand."

He chuckled as he sat back and studied me. "When Jet came asking questions about the fire that claimed Alpha Kyle, Luna Brooke, and their children, I was surprised to be told that he suspected that the daughter somehow survived the event."

"They didn't die in a fire, and you knew Carly was alive. That is why you had a tracker nosing around." Mom snapped.

The smile Kain gave mom made him look purely evil. He didn't respond to mom and turned back to me. "Jet wanted to know if there was a chance that his little sister's daughter might have survived. Don't worry, we told him there was no possible way."

"Jet is my uncle?" I asked quietly. I hadn't really thought about that. Mom had said that my birth mother was the daughter of the Alpha King, but I hadn't made the connection yet.

Kain looked at me like I was stupid before looking at mom. "Have you not told her anything?" he asked before turning back to me. "Your mother," He sneered. "Was the daughter of the Alpha King, making you, his granddaughter. My dear, you are one of the strongest wolves out there.

Stronger than even your mother or Jet. Your blood not only holds that of the Alpha King, but also of one of the strongest Alpha lines in the kingdom. That is why you will be my son's mate."

Mom yelled and lunged for Kain. She dove over the desk as Kain stood. She managed to get a few well-placed punches to his face before he plunged a dagger into her heart, and I screamed. I tried to get to mom's slumped body, but a guard grabbed me around my waist. I continued to scream as I was hauled from the room.

The guard carried me upstairs to the second floor. I continued to try to fight against him, but I was no match for him. He opened a door, and I was shoved inside before the door was slammed closed.

I heard the lock engage and I fell to the ground sobbing. He had killed her. He had killed mom.

I moved to the far corner of the room before sitting and pulling my knees to my chest. I didn't know what to do. I was completely on my own with a mad man. And I had no idea where I was. *"Is there even a point in fighting this anymore?"* I sobbed.

"Don't think like that!" Cora yelled at me. *"We are strong, and we will get through this."* She too had tears in her eyes.

"How, Cora? How are we supposed to get out of here?" I snapped at her. *"The guys here look like the Hulk, Kain is certifiably nuts, and mom is dead."*

"I don't know yet." Cora said. *"But I can't have you giving up on us."*

I nodded and wiped my cheeks. There would be plenty of time to grieve mom after we got out of here, and I would get out of here.

Several hours passed before a man entered the room. When he saw me in the corner, he stopped. A look of surprise crossed his face before he masked it. "You must be Carly." He said calmly as he moved to a door to his right.

He was in there for a few minutes before reappearing in a suit. "Alpha Kain is anxious for us to meet him downstairs, so I am going to need you to get dressed. Your clothes are waiting in the bathroom. You have ten minutes." he said in a bored tone as he sat on the bed.

I slowly got to my feet and walked to the bathroom. I closed and locked the door behind me. Hanging on the back of the door was a beautiful white dress. My mouth dropped open as I stared at the garment.

"Is that a wedding dress?" I asked Cora.

"It sure looks like one." She responded. I hesitated, not wanting to put it on. *"Unfortunately, I don't see another option."*

I grimaced as I pulled the dress on. It was floor length with a slit that stopped mid-thigh, cap sleeved and exactly my size. I zipped up the back and used my fingers to comb through my hair. There was a pair of heels on the floor, and I slipped them on. All in all, the dress and the heels were beautiful.

I looked down at myself and sighed. At least I had my workout shorts on under my jeans when I was captured. I hated how vulnerable dresses made me feel. With shorts on, I felt a little more covered. I took a deep breath and stepped back into the room.

The man was still on the bed. He had his phone out and he looked like he was texting. I took a moment to observe him. He had light brown hair and brown eyes. He was about six feet tall and looked thin but fit. He glanced up at me with indifference before setting his phone down next to him.

"What is it you want?" He asked, as if I had chosen to be here.

"Excuse me?" I asked in irritation. "It's not like I want to be here."

He raised his brow in surprise before standing. "My father told me you came here to unite yourself with me."

I laughed. "Is that so? Well, your dad is a nutcase who kidnapped me and killed my mother in front of me." I glared at him. "I will not be aligning myself with you. I would rather die."

The man smiled in relief, and I was momentarily shocked into silence. "That is what I had hoped to hear." The man ran his hand through his hair. "My name is Kion, Kain's son." He gave a small bow. "I am going to be honest with you, cousin, I have a mate and don't want anyone else."

"Then why am I here?" I crossed my arms over my chest.

"My father has threatened to kill my mate if I do not mark you." Kion said quickly. "I can't let anything happen to her. I love her. But my father has it in his head that you are the only one for me. From the time I was small he has been telling me that I will be with you. Then I met my mate on the day of my eighteenth birthday." He swallowed hard. "I need your help to keep her safe."

"How can I do that?" I asked suspiciously.

Kion glanced at the door before stepping in my direction and lowering his voice. "I am having a witch's potion made. This potion makes a mating mark temporary for three days. The mark has to be given within an hour of taking the potion."

I blinked at him. "I have never met you in my life. Your father has kidnapped me to force me to marry you. Now you want me to drink some witch's potion and allow you to mark me? How do I know this isn't a trick to get me to willingly let you mark me?"

"I understand you do not trust me; you have no reason to. But if you don't, my mate is going to die." I could see the pleading in his eyes as he stared at me.

"I think he is telling the truth." Cora said. *"But I still don't like the idea of him marking us, even though it will be temporary."*

"This temporary marking, will there be any side effects to it? Will we really be mated for those three days?" I watched him carefully, trying to see if I could sense any signs of deception.

"No, from what the witch said, the only things that will happen is my scent will be on you and the visible mark. We won't be connected in any other way." He said with sincerity.

I sighed and shook my head. I can't believe I am agreeing to this. "When are we supposed to be marking each other?"

Kion's sense of relief was palpable. "I'm not sure. We are supposed to head down to dinner in a few minutes. The potion should be ready a little later tonight." Kion looked down at the ground before looking back at me with a sad look. "I'm sorry about your parents and your mom. I wish I could somehow bring them back."

My vision blurred with tears. Kion walked over to me and pulled me into a side hug. I was surprised by his show of compassion. Cora bristled a little, but neither of us felt threatened by Kion. I truly believed that he was just as much a victim in his dad's plot as I was.

A knock came at the door, and it opened to reveal two of the hulking guards. Kion offered his arm to me. I hesitantly took it, allowing Kion to lead me out into the hall. One guard was in front of us and the other in back. Apparently, Kain thought of us as a flight risk.

We descended to the ground floor and then entered a large banquet hall. The whole room was filled with flowers, white drapes, and candles. Tons of people were conversing in small groups, but when we were noticed, a hush fell around the room. Kain stood from his place at the front of the room with a large smile.

"Here they are." Kain called. "Now the ceremony can begin." Kion tensed as the guards nudged us forward. I could hear his rapidly beating heart. It matched my own.

My mind was frantically searching for a way out of this. The witch's potion was my only chance to not be permanently marked by Kion, now that Kain was pushing a Binding Ceremony.

A small movement caught my eye. A young woman stood off to the side with a pained expression as she watched us, and I wondered if she was Kion's mate. Her eyes flicked to the two wine glasses in her hands full of a dark red liquid. I don't know how, but I knew that they held the witch's potion.

I tightened my hand on Kion's arm, and he looked at me before following my gaze. His body relaxed when he saw the woman and then tensed again.

We reached Kain and he put a hand on both of our shoulders, turning us to face the crowd. His grip on me was painful and I winced. How was I going to get the potion? "Today we are gathered together to celebrate my son, Kion and his mate Carly." I coughed a few times, and he gave me a hard look. He squeezed my shoulder even harder and I whimpered softly. "The Binding Ceremony will take place followed by them marking one another." He announced.

I started coughing again as an older man stepped up to take Kain's position in front of us. "Are you okay?" Kion whispered in concern. I stopped coughing and gave him a nod.

The older man began the ceremony, and I would periodically start coughing throughout it. Each time I would cough, the man would pause the ceremony until I stopped. Kain grew increasingly irritated with me, but Kion grew more and more concerned. I had been to a few Binding Ceremonies over the years, and something seemed off with this one. The wording didn't sound quite right. Right before the man invited us to mark each other, I started my worst coughing fit yet.

"Someone, get this girl something to drink!" Kain roared.

The young woman I had seen with the wine glasses earlier rushed up and handed me one of the glasses. Her face remained expressionless, but her eyes smiled. "Thank you." I croaked, just for good measure.

I downed the whole glass before handing it back. The potion was awful, and I did my best not to make a face at the horrible taste. She gave me a small smile and a quick nod before Kain shooed her away.

"Now, can they mark each other?" Kain growled. The man nodded nervously and Kain gave Kion a shove towards me.

He nervously stepped up to me. I saw his eyes move to something over my shoulder before he took a deep breath. I felt his warm breath on my neck. His teeth barely broke the skin before pain shot through my neck. My vision blurred as the pain became more intense.

Kion took a step back and studied my face. The pain and nausea had me doubling over. I started to dry-heave as sweat broke out on my forehead. Kion put an arm around me to keep me standing. I heard people yelling and someone helping me walk. My vision was so blurry, I couldn't even tell where we were going.

We eventually stopped moving and someone pulled my hair back into a ponytail. I was lowered to the ground as a cool rag was laid on the back of my neck and over the mark.

After a while the pain subsided, and my vision cleared. I was sitting on the bathroom floor with Kion pacing the small space and the young woman with the wine glasses was sitting next to me.

"Wow, that potion sure packed a punch." I groaned.

"I'm so sorry, I couldn't warn you about the potential side effects." The woman said. "Your body seems to be rejecting the mark."

"Good. I don't want it." I said as I looked at her. "I only allowed it because of the threat to you."

She looked at me in confusion before looking up at Kion. "What is she talking about?"

"You are Kion's mate, are you not?" I looked at her, confused as well.

"Mary, my dad was going to kill you if I didn't mark Carly." Kion knelt in front of Mary and took her face in his hands. "I couldn't let that happen. That is why we needed the potion."

"Kion." Mary said anxiously. "Carly is now the one in danger."

"What do you mean?" Kion asked. "The potion makes it so the mark only lasts for three days."

Mary shook her head. "I talked with a second witch. Magic is rarely as simple as the first one claimed it was. She told me that the mark would be temporary for three days, but if Carly's mate doesn't mark her in that time, she will die." Kion groaned, but Mary continued. "The mark you gave her will not heal and will start bleeding at the end of day three. Nothing can stop it. The witch said if her body rejects the marking, each day at the time she was marked, she will go through the same pain she did receiving it."

"We need to leave tonight. All three of us." Kion said as he stood. "Do you know who your mate is?" He asked me. I shook my head, and he ran his hands through his hair. "We will head back to the Silver Moon Pack, then. Mary, stay with Carly and I will get things ready."

Kion left and I laid down on the floor. Mary continued to change out the cool rags frequently to help soothe my heated skin. I was in and out while they were making plans and gathering things.

"Cora?" I asked softly.

"I'm here, Carly."

"What are the odds we will find our mate?" I asked as I closed my eyes.

"I have no idea, but the odds don't seem good." she said sadly.

I sighed as I listened to Mary and Kion speaking quietly as they prepared for us to escape. My neck still burned, but at least I wasn't going to pass out from it. Cora whined in pain as well. It felt like fire licking up the side of my neck.

Neither Cora nor I regretted taking the potion. We would rather die than be mated to someone who we did not choose. And if we were going to die, it was nice to know that we were able to help two people who needed it.

Chapter 14

Mary had gone back to the witch and acquired a spray that would mask our scents for a few days. Kion held Mary's hand as we snuck through the halls of the North Wind packhouse. They frequently glanced back at me to make sure I was still following them. Once outside, we slowed our pace and moved in the shadows. We had been walking for several miles before Kion let us stop for a break.

Kion looked behind us and a sad look crossed his face. He took a deep breath. "I, Kion Johnson, reject Alpha Kain as my Alpha and break any and all ties I have to the North Wind Pack."

Mary moved to Kion's side and slipped her hand in his. "I, Mary Howard, reject Alpha Kain as my Alpha and break any and all ties I have to the North Wind Pack."

Kion smiled down at Mary before kissing her. I looked away to give them some privacy. A minute later Kion spoke quietly. "We should get going. My father would have felt us breaking ties with him and the pack. He will not be happy and will most likely try to hunt us down."

I nodded and we began moving again. Our pace was faster than before, no doubt because Kain now knew we were missing. We kept going until the sky started to lighten with the rising sun.

Kion found a cave for us to rest in and we all gratefully collapsed once inside. My feet were killing me. I hadn't thought about changing my shoes before our escape and these heels weren't exactly comfortable for running and hiking. I glanced across the cave as I rubbed my feet. I watched as Kion wrapped his arms around Mary, and she snuggled into him. My heart hurt thinking of all the times Easton had put his arms around me. I closed my eyes and tried to block thoughts of him. I needed to focus on escaping and I needed to sleep while I could.

We only slept for a few hours before we were moving again. This time we were traveling as wolves. Cora was elated to be running and we enjoyed the sensation of running as a wolf. My senses were heightened, and the world looked so different from Cora's perspective.

It had been twenty-four hours since Kion marked me when pain spread from the mark. I collapsed to the earth while Kion and Mary's wolves whined nearby. After several minutes, the pain finally faded enough for us to keep going.

We rested for a few minutes more before traveling again. I felt weaker. Kion kept a closer eye on me while Mary stayed close to my side. It was comforting to know that they were here with me. It helped Cora and I stay focused on moving forward.

Over the last few days, we had all become close. Kion became a pseudo brother of sorts. He remembered a few things about us as children and happily shared the stories. He was more serious than Max, Easton, and Mike, but he was kind and protective. He would make a great leader if he ever wanted to rise up the ranks of whatever pack they ended up in. Mary was sweet and nurturing. The two of them together were perfect.

Day two was coming to a close as the sun was sinking low in the sky. Kion came to an abrupt halt. His wolf scanned the area on high alert. He began to growl as he took up a protective stance in front of Mary and me.

My heart rate picked up speed as I saw close to fifty wolves stepping out of the trees on the other side of the meadow. They hadn't seemed to know we were there until Kion growled. All of them turned to look at us. Had Kain gotten in front of us already? Mary whimpered and Kion moved again to block her more from the threat.

The wolves in front of us were definitely approaching aggressively. *"I don't like this, Carly."* Cora growled. *"There has to be a way to resolve this confrontation without actually fighting. We will be slaughtered."*

"We need to show them that we are not a threat." I told her.

A breeze blew across the clearing. The scent of sandalwood filled my nose and drew my attention. I couldn't tell where it was coming from. I shook my head to refocus on the task at hand. I nudged Kion's leg with my head before moving forward. He snapped at my tail to try to get me to stop, but he missed, and I continued.

Ten of the closest wolves approached quickly. Two branched off and headed for me while the others ran past, heading for Kion and Mary. I growled and tackled a dark grey wolf with a lighter ear. I hit him so hard that we rolled several feet. I dashed away before coming back for another attack.

The other wolves had stopped their advance on Kion and Mary and turned toward me and their companion. I noted their slow approach and that they were attempting to create a circle around us.

I sprinted for the dark grey wolf. I could see him brace, waiting for me to hit his side, so I jumped over his back and kicked his other side causing the wolf to fall again. I turned on him, baring my teeth. No one was going to hurt my friends. Cora and I would fight to the death to protect Kion and Mary. The wolf was growling as we circled each other. I noticed he had dark green eyes and for a moment I thought of Easton.

"Carly?" I whipped my head around and saw Papa Bear standing with the wolves that had surrounded us. I whimpered and ran for him, knocking him to the ground. I rubbed my head against him with my tail wagging. "How are you a wolf?" he asked in a hoarse whisper.

I jumped off him and shifted back to human. While I shifted, he got to his feet. As soon as I was back to my human self, I threw my arms around him and started to cry. He held me close and whispered soothing words while stroking my hair.

"I'm sorry." I said as I stepped back and wiped my eyes. "What are you doing here? How are you here?" I asked, looking around. All the wolves had moved closer, and several had shifted back to their human forms.

Holly pulled me into a tight hug. "We have been following your scent for weeks, hun." She released me, wiping away her own tears.

"What is that on your neck?" Jason said angrily as he turned my head to the side. "Who marked you?" He growled before his eyes snapped to Kion.

Kion and Mary stood off to the side holding hands. When Jason started to advance on Kion, I tried to grab his arm to stop him, but he shook me off. Papa Bear was on a war path. I ran and stood in front of him. "Stop, you don't understand!" I yelled, but he tried to shove me aside. Kion pushed Mary behind him in order to protect her.

I growled and threw my fist as hard as I could into Jason's face. He stumbled back a few feet. I shook out my hand as I glared at him. "Carly?" he asked in confusion.

"I swear, you touch him, and I will…" Pain shot through my neck, and I screamed as I dropped to my knees, holding my hand over the mark. The pain was getting worse each time. My vision started to fade from the intensity of it.

"Carly, day two is done." Mary was at my side with her arms protectively around me.

"I know." I ground out.

"What is going on?" Alpha Callum called over several people yelling. There were several guys holding another one back, but my eyes wouldn't focus.

Kion moved to stand in front of me. "Alpha, it's all my fault. Carly is in danger because of me."

"No." I said through clenched teeth. "I did this willingly."

"Just for the record, what did you do willingly?" Alpha Callum asked.

"Alpha Kain was forcing them to mark each other. If they refused, he would kill me. Carly took a witch's potion to prevent Kion's mark from sticking." Mary said as she helped me lay down on the grass. The pain was finally subsiding. "We were unaware of a condition that the potion had, until it was too late."

After several minutes the pain had mostly faded, and I slowly sat back up. I got to my feet and wobbled. A strong arm wrapped around me to keep me steady. Sandalwood flooded my senses as warmth spread through my body. I looked up to see Easton looking at me anxiously. Tears blurred my vision as I wrapped my arms around his neck. He held me tightly to him.

"What condition?" he asked softly as he pulled me closer.

"When was she marked?" I heard Jason ask.

"I marked her two days ago." Kion said.

Easton's arms tightened around me. I let go of his neck, sliding my hands down his chest as I turned slightly to look at those gathering around us.

"How did you know I was here?" I asked.

"I got the most terrifying voicemail. I heard Dax attack you in your kitchen and then I heard them take you away." Easton buried his face in my neck, and I shivered at the contact. He let out a low growl that was barely audible.

"What we heard in that voicemail was bad." Max agreed. "When we got back to the house, the front door was broken open and there was only one scent there. I had never smelled it before, but Easton said it was yours, so we gathered some of our best warriors and started to follow it. We came across Jet and several of his men along the way. He offered to help us get you back."

I looked over the faces around me. Alpha Callum, Gamma Jason, Gamma Holly, and Mike were all there too. Many of the others I had seen around the pack, but there were more that I didn't recognize. Jet also stood not far off. He was watching me carefully to see my reaction. I turned to face him, and I felt Easton's arms lower.

"Do I really look like my mother?" I asked.

A sad smile formed on his lips. "All except your eyes, those are your father's. You fight like her too. She didn't like to fight, but if she felt there was no other choice, she was a force."

"I'm sorry to whoever I tackled." I said sheepishly.

Easton grabbed my hand and gave it a squeeze. A tingling sensation spread up my arm along with the warmth that usually accompanied Easton's touch. "I forgive you." I turned to look at him. "So, you shifted that night. It wasn't just being overwhelmed."

"Yeah, I'm sorry for lying to you." I looked down. "Cora and I felt like we needed to keep it a secret until mom was found."

"Where is your mother?" Alpha Callum asked. "And who are these two?"

"This is Kion, Kain's son, who also happens to be my cousin. And this is Mary, his mate." I introduced them.

I swallowed hard as the images of mom having a knife in her chest flooded back into my mind. I had been suppressing the memories for the past several days, focusing on survival. Now that I was safe, they came back in a rush.

"Kain killed her mom in front of her two days ago." Kion told the group as he moved to my side before pulling me into a hug.

A loud growl came from behind me, and I turned to see Easton with a murderous expression on his face. His green eyes were so dark they looked almost black. "Easton?" I asked softly, but his whole focus was on Kion.

Mike chuckled. "If I were you, I would unhand Carly." Kion slowly removed his arms from around me and stepped back, hands raised.

"What the heck is going on?" I asked, irritated. I crossed my arms over my chest and looked around. Jet had an amused smile on his face, Jason and Holly watched Easton with surprise, Mike and Max were grinning ear to ear, Alpha Callum had a thoughtful expression. I turned my attention back to Easton, whose eyes were lightening to their normal color. "I'm really not in the mood for more crap-tastic news."

"No way!" Cora said quietly. *"No freaking way! Easton is our mate!"* She yelled as she jumped around in excitement.

I cocked my head to the side as I looked Easton up and down. His hair was disheveled, and it looked like he hadn't shaved in weeks. He watched me warily for a few minutes before taking a step towards me. I took a step back. Pain flashed through his expression, but he stopped moving towards me. The scent of sandalwood had grown stronger when he had moved closer.

"I can't believe he is our mate." I said to Cora. *"Why didn't he tell us? Is this why we have been so drawn to him?"*

Cora growled. *"And why he didn't take our promise seriously and asked to be the exception."* She did not like being played with. *"Oh, no. He needs to know he is not allowed to walk all over us."* Cora said. *"He needs to treat us with a little more respect than that."*

I lifted the skirt of my dirty dress, turned on my heels and ran. I wasn't running fast, I wanted him to catch up, but I also wanted to tire him out. And I didn't want anyone around to see us when we finally confronted each other. I heard him coming up behind me. I let him tackle me from behind. He had turned so his body took most of the fall. I rolled out of his arms.

"Carly, we need to talk about this." He said as he got to his feet breathing hard. "Please."

Cora surged forward and took control. She started to throw punches. He blocked them easily. I could tell when he realized it wasn't me that was fighting him.

"Cora, I'm not going to fight you." He said calmly, which only angered her more.

"How long did you know?" Cora yelled as my elbow connected with his abdomen. He groaned and bent forward.

"Cora, please let me talk with Carly. I promise I will answer all your questions." Easton begged as he slowly straightened back up. He was watching me warily.

Cora growled, but stepped back so that I could be in control again. She paced in the back of my mind, still fuming. "How long, Easton?" I asked as I crossed my arms over my chest.

He looked marginally relieved that I was back in control. "Since the day at the waterfall. I saw you talking with three guys, and I was angry that you were talking with them. Then Dax grabbed you and you tried to get away from him. I wanted to rip his head off for touching you. When you bumped into me as you backed away from Dax, I caught a hint of your scent. It was intoxicating and I knew you were my mate. Then I saw Dax eyeing you in those shorts you were wearing. I put my shirt on you so no one would see you." Easton ran his hand through his hair.

I turned my back to him and took a deep breath. I heard him slowly approaching, but I didn't look at him. He slid his arms around me.

"Carly, if I could have told you, I would have. I almost did several times. After Max danced with you. After meeting up with Dax again on the way back to your house. After you undressed to climb the side of your house. After seeing you get beat up in class because of my idiocy. After your fight with Jet." He pressed a kiss to my shoulder. "Seeing you sick was complete torture. Every time we touched, I caught a faint hint of your scent, but as soon as I let you go, I couldn't really smell it anymore. You have been driving me crazy, Carr." He pressed a kiss to my neck. "Then we spent lunch together and I couldn't hold back anymore. Carly, I need you."

I turned in his arms and looked up into his eyes. He was pleading with me to understand, to forgive him. "Why did you growl at Kion? He was only trying to comfort me. He feels somewhat guilty because his dad was the one who killed my mom." I asked, searching his face for answers.

"His scent is all over you, Carly. His mark is on your neck where mine should be. You are mine, not his. He has no business touching you." Easton's arms tightened around me, and his eyes darkened as he buried his face in my neck. His body tensed. "Carly, I can't handle this. His scent is all over you and all I want to do is hurt him." Easton's grip on me slackened as he tried to take a step away. I put my arms around his neck and held him in place. His eyes were still dark and filled with a fierceness that surprised me.

I rose on my toes and pressed my lips to his. It took him a few seconds before he returned the kiss. This time it was fierce and possessive. His hand tangled in my hair, and he held me close. We were both out of breath by the time we pulled apart for air. Easton rested his forehead against mine. "I still want to hurt him."

I laughed and kissed him again. Then I sobered. "We need to get back to the others." I said as I turned to head back the way we had come. Easton grabbed my hand and pulled me back to him. He kissed me again and I smiled against his lips.

"Now that you know that we are mates, I plan on kissing you a lot more." Easton warned as he led the way. "That promise you and Cora made was about my undoing."

"And what of you?" I asked, and he glanced back at me in confusion. "I saw you in the hall with Marissa."

Easton whirled on me and pinned me against a nearby tree before kissing me with a determination that stole my breath. He pulled back and looked me in the eye. "Understand this Carly, you have always and will always be the only woman for me. And I have always been yours. The kiss during lunch was the first time I ever kissed anyone, and I don't plan on kissing anyone but you. Marissa latched herself onto me and she got written up for inappropriate behavior." This time when we kissed it was sweet and full of promise.

Chapter 15

We entered the clearing hand in hand. Tents had been set up around the area and men were cooking over campfires. Those who saw us gave us smiles as we passed. Easton entered a large tent near the center of the camp. Alpha Callum, Gamma Jason, Jet, Mike, Max, and Kion were standing there talking about Kain. When we entered, all attention turned to us.

"Not even a black eye? I'm a little disappointed in you, Carly." Max smiled as he walked over. He gave me a hug and Easton growled.

I elbowed him in the ribs to get him to stop. "Sorry. It's his scent on you, its driving me crazy." Easton grumbled.

"About that." Kion folded his arms over his chest. "Carly has less than twenty-four hours before she dies."

The occupants of the tent went silent. "Way to sugar coat my fate." I shot a glare at him.

"It had to be said, Carly. Your family has the right to know." Kion shrugged off my glare.

"What do you mean she has less than twenty-four hours to live?" Easton asked. He put his arms protectively around me and glared at Kion like he was the one who was going to murder me.

"Are you Carly's mate?" Kion asked. "Only her true mate can save her."

Easton pulled me closer to him, shielding me partially from Kion. "She is mine." He growled.

"Good." Kion said simply. "Mark her."

"What? You want Easton to mark Carly while your mark is already on her?" Mike asked, getting angry. "It would be excruciating to have a mark given over another mark. It doesn't even look like it is close to healing. She might not live through it."

"I'm sure it will be excruciating. But if her true mate doesn't mark her by the end of day three after the first marking, she will bleed out and die." Kion countered. "The mark is already starting to bleed a little and she has been getting weaker each day."

I raised my hand to my neck and pulled it away. There was a small amount of blood on my fingers. I leaned into Easton, and I could feel him looking at me. He tilted my chin up, forcing me to meet his gaze. He was worried. He didn't bother hiding it.

"Carly, I won't force my mark on you." He said quietly. "I will only mark you if that is what you want." I nodded and he pressed a kiss to my forehead. "How bad is the pain going to be?" He asked those gathered.

"She nearly passed out when she received mine and I barely broke through the skin, so probably worse than that." Kion responded.

Alpha Callum stepped forward. "Would you two like to have a wedding along with the Binding Ceremony?"

Easton looked down at me and I nodded. "Yes, sir. If Carly is to wear my mark, I want her as my wife as well." Easton replied.

Ten minutes later, I was standing with Easton in front of Alpha Callum. Easton held tightly to my hand as we were married, and the Binding Ceremony took place. I noticed several key things that were left out of the Binding Ceremony I had with Kion.

All one hundred and ten warriors cheered as we made our way back to the Alpha's tent. Alpha Callum had suggested we do the marking alone, since it was going to be extremely painful. I grew anxious as we drew closer to the tent.

Once we were inside, Easton pulled me to him and kissed me. He leaned back and looked at me with a worried expression. He gently stroked my cheek. "You ready, sweetheart?" he asked softly.

I shook my head. "Not really, but we really don't have a choice."

"We'll get through this together." He kissed me softly. "Why don't you mark me first?" Easton suggested.

Easton's arms around me tightened as I sunk my canines into his neck. Cora had made sure it was extra deep and more painful than it needed to be. Easton laid his forehead on my shoulder as he breathed deeply through the pain. "Sorry." I gave him an apologetic smile. "Cora is still a little mad at you."

When he recovered, he straightened up. "I'm sure she isn't the only one still mad at me." He pressed a kiss to the tip of my nose. "But I plan on doing my best to make up for everything." He gave me a crooked grin before giving me a light kiss on the lips. Easton pressed feather light kisses along my jaw before stopping at the spot where he had given me a hickey before. "There is still a faint mark here." Easton said quietly.

"Yeah, your mark." I laughed lightly. I felt him smile against my skin and he moved to the place he needed to mark. I tensed, knowing how painful the last time had been.

Easton paused with his lips brushing the skin on my neck. "I love you, Carly." He whispered before he bit down. Pain exploded through my neck at the same time warmth spread through me. I felt Easton holding me tight. I buried my face in his neck and held onto him like he alone could save me from this pain. I bit my cheek to try to prevent a scream from escaping but it didn't work. This was way worse than Kion's. My vision began to fade, and I whimpered. "I love you, Sweetheart. I'm so sorry." Easton's voice sounded far away as blackness enveloped me.

*   *   *

I groaned as I tried to force my eyes open. I buried my face into my pillow as I tried to sit up. "Relax, Sweetheart." Easton's voice was soft. A hand gently combed through my hair. "Take it slow." I took a deep breath, and my senses were filled with sandalwood. Easton.

I was curled up beside him with my head on his chest. I turned and looked up at him confused about how I had gotten there. "Good morning." I mumbled.

Easton chuckled before pressing a kiss to my forehead. "More like good afternoon, Love."

Love? I closed my eyes as memories came back to me. Coming across the army. Finding out Easton was my mate. The witch's potion. Easton and I having a Binding Ceremony. Marking each other. I opened my eyes again and saw his smiling face with his dimple making an appearance.

"How long was I out?" I asked.

Easton brushed the hair back from my face. "A day and a half. How are you feeling?"

"Would you believe me if I told you that I felt warm?" I said as I snuggled closer to him. Easton laughed as his arms tightened around me. "And a little sore."

"I bet you are sore. The pain you were in…" His voice trailed off and he pressed a kiss to my head. "I don't think I could handle seeing you like that again." He cleared his throat after a few moments. "And I told you, your own personal heater would be nice."

I looked back up at him and smiled. Before I could say anything, the flap of the tent was flipped up and Max walked in. He stopped and looked at me before sticking his head back out of the tent.

"Sleeping Beauty is finally awake!" Max yelled.

"I think that is our cue to get up." I whispered to Easton before pressing a quick kiss to his lips. I sat up and stretched. My neck felt tight and sore, but everything else seemed to be fine. "Worried that much about me, Max?" I asked him as I slowly stood.

Max glared at me. "You were screaming in agony for hours. The whole camp was concerned. Only Easton could touch you without you thrashing around even more."

I looked between Max and Easton as he stood from the cot we were laying on. "That bad?" I asked.

"Worse." Easton rubbed a hand over his face. The dark circles under his eyes were a testament to the little sleep he had gotten. "You finally stopped only a few hours ago." I wrapped my arms around his neck and kissed him gently.

"Just think of it this way." I said as I pulled back and headed for the door of the tent. "If I hadn't gone through that, I would be bleeding out right now and you would be watching me slowly die."

"That's not funny." Max and Easton said in unison, and I laughed.

Jason and Mike were jogging in our direction. When Mike saw me, he broke out into a run. He nearly knocked me to the ground as he hugged me. Easton gave a warning growl and I laughed, returning Mike's hug.

"Good to see you, too." I said with a smile.

I think they all missed us. Cora laughed.

"What has everyone been up to?" I asked, stepping back and immediately Easton's arms came around me from behind. "I feel like I haven't seen you all in ages."

Mike shook his head. "We have been looking for you. What I want to know is what happened to you for the two weeks you were gone."

"I agree." Jason said, folding his arms over his chest. "Why don't you tell us everything while you eat something."

Easton released me and grabbed my hand as we followed his dad to a large campfire where Alpha Callum, Gamma Holly, and Jet were sitting. They all smiled at me as we approached. Easton sat on the ground with his back against a log and extended his arm in invitation to sit next to him. I ignored his gesture and kicked his foot a little before sitting between his legs and leaning back against him. He laughed and wrapped his arms around me.

"I could get use to this." He whispered in my ear before pressing a kiss to my cheek.

"You two are nauseating." Max shook his head in mock disgust as he handed me a bowl of soup.

Mike laughed. "But East was right. I don't know how, but he was right."

"Right about what?" Jet asked, intrigued.

"From the day we first met Carly, Easton had been adamant that she was his." Max said with a smile.

"We were walking back to the packhouse and Easton warned us to stay away from her because he fully believed she was his mate." Mike continued.

"Then he fought with any boy that looked at her too long or said anything negative about her. Poor Benson had been traumatized when Easton attacked him when we were eight." Max added.

"At least he learned to control his temper as we grew up." Mike commented.

"You call making sure that he was next to her whenever possible so that none of the guys would approach her, learning control? Or the fact that he punched me more than once, control?" Max scoffed. "Then we got home from camp, and he realized she really was his mate. He became doubly protective of her. Even asked us to keep an eye on her at school."

"You knew she was your mate when you were five?" Jason asked in surprise. Easton adjusted his position behind me allowing me to lean back more.

"I wouldn't call it knowing she was my mate. I just had an overwhelming need to protect her, and I got angry when anyone looked at her." Easton shrugged.

"And what of you, Carly? Did you experience something similar?" Jet asked as he watched us closely.

"I have always been drawn to him. I don't think I would have come out of hiding if Easton hadn't been there that day at the waterfall." I furrowed my brow in thought. "Then he started teasing me mercilessly and I felt betrayed and picked on. I started to avoid him, Max, and Mike at all costs. Mom said I was taking it too hard. I somehow knew whenever he was getting close and could hide somewhere until he was gone. Then he left for camp.

"At the waterfall, when Dax showed up, I was changing and literally in only my bra and shorts." Easton's stiffened behind me. "I put my shirt on and then East and Max showed up. I was more nervous about them than Dax and his goons. Then Easton put his shirt on me, and I felt confused and oddly comforted. It was weird. Everything seemed to change after that. Whenever Easton touched me, my anxiety and worries would go away." I shrugged and took a sip of my soup.

"When did you shift, Easton?" Jet asked.

"A few days after getting to camp." Easton answered.

Jet let out a laugh of disbelief. "Do you realize how rare of a bond you have? To recognize each other as your mate as children is impressive."

"That and Carly could talk to her wolf since she was sixteen. That is impressive too." Max added with a shake of his head.

"Wait, what?" Holly asked.

"Thanks, Max." I muttered. Seeing everyone staring at me, I sighed. "On my sixteenth birthday I could talk with Cora."

"Carly, when Easton returned from camp, your wolf was probably sensing more of the mate bond since Easton had his wolf." Jet said while rubbing his jaw. "But you should have been able to recognize him as your mate immediately."

"I couldn't see Cora or shift or use any of my wolf senses." I said quietly before I looked down at my wrist. I took off my bracelet and lifted it to get a better look at it. "I wonder if this had anything to do with it."

"You always had this on. When we were young, I always wanted to take it off of you. Conall even wanted me to remove it from your wrist as soon as we saw you at the banquet." Easton said as he gently touched the chain. "What is it?"

I let him take it. "It was used to mask my scent so that the North Wind Pack couldn't find us. Well, this was mom's, mine I think is back at the house. I took it off and switched it for mom's. They are specific to us. I put on hers so that they would think my scent was still being masked."

"Wouldn't Dax be able to smell you?" Jason asked.

"He would have if I hadn't booby trapped the front door." I shrugged. "As soon as he broke in, a powder fell on him and his guys, causing them to go nose blind."

Easton chuckled and kissed my cheek. "So that is what all the red powder was in the entryway." I nodded.

"The bracelet not only masked my scent but dulled my werewolf side. That is why I was weaker than everyone else. I would easily get sick, and I was cold constantly." I explained.

"Yet, you still beat me." Jet commented. "Carly, do you know your lineage?" When I nodded, he continued. "As a member of the royal family, you still shift at eighteen but your connection to your wolf can start early. Not every royal does, only the strongest seem to have that ability. Your mother was the only one of the Alpha King's three children to get their wolf early."

"Carly is related to the Alpha King?" Max exclaimed in surprise.

"My younger sister, Brooke, married Alpha Kyle of the North Wind Pack. Carly is their firstborn. We were told the entire Alpha family was killed in a fire shortly after Kyle and Brooke announced the upcoming birth of a son." Jet explained.

"But that wasn't true." Kion's voice had everyone turning to look at him. He stood with his arm around Mary. He had a grim look on his face. "Dad sent mom and me to a friend's house on the far side of the pack. I overheard him and some men talking about getting rid of the obstacles that stood in the way of him and his bloodline being Alpha. The next morning, we got word that Alpha Kyle, Luna Brooke, and Carly were killed in a fire. The pack was devastated by their deaths." Kion shook his head. "Dad became angry a week later after some of his closest men met with him. When I asked him what was wrong, he told me my mate was missing, but he had a plan to bring her back."

"Savannah saved me with the help of a witch to mask our scents." I picked up the story. "She said we tried to stay with her sister, but North Wind Pack members were nosing around, and we ran again. We lived as rogues for over a year, constantly moving from place to place." Easton's arms around me tightened briefly.

"Then a little girl came out of the waterfall and started to play with our boys." Holly said, wiping tears from her face. "Why didn't your mom or Savannah or…" Holly furrowed her brow confused as to what to call the woman who had been pretending to be my mother for fifteen years.

"Savannah raised and protected me. She is my mom." I said quietly.

"She did tell me, Harry, and Jason that Carly was in danger from her previous pack several weeks ago." Alpha Callum said. "But she didn't mention which pack or that Carly was the Alpha King's granddaughter."

I looked at him and understanding dawned. Mom's talk with Alpha and Jason. Mom's tense behavior when Jet showed up. It all started to fall into place. Mom had done everything in her power to keep me safe. Even told Alpha about us being in hiding because she knew she was going to have to go away on an assignment.

"Carly, she was a hero." Cora said softly.

"I know, Cora." I said, fighting back tears.

Easton must have sensed my emotional shift. He lifted me so that I was sitting on his lap with my legs off to the side. I rested my head on his shoulder as his arms came back around me. He held me close as I listened to the conversation around us.

I was almost asleep when Alpha Callum asked me a question. "Carly, I know you have been through a lot over the past several weeks. We heard the voicemail and have a pretty good idea of what happened when they took you, but can you tell us what happened after they did?"

I didn't bother sitting up or lifting my head. I stayed snuggled up against Easton. "I do not remember a whole lot. They kept me drugged until a few days ago. Whenever I woke up, someone would give me another injection of something. The last time I woke up, they were dumping me into a room. They brought mom in a while later and she told me everything about our escape from the North Wind Pack. The next morning, they took us down to an office. I punched Dax in the face when he shoved me into the room." Max and Mike chuckled.

"I'm pretty sure Kain killed Dax because he demanded more money. He said I was difficult to manage, which is the farthest thing from the truth. I am an angel." Jason chuckled while Max, Easton, and Mike laughed.

"I can't imagine you being difficult, Carly." Max said sarcastically.

Easton pressed a kiss to my cheek. "What happened next, my angel?"

"Kain told me I would be his son's mate. Mom got mad and tried to attack Kain. He stabbed her in the heart." I swallowed hard. "I was immediately taken up to a different room."

"I was surprised to see you in my bedroom." Kion said. "We got dressed for dinner and…"

"You got dressed in his room with him?" Easton cut in. I could feel his anger radiating off of him.

"I dressed in the bathroom with the door locked." I clarified. "It's not like you have room to talk. I was in a towel and underwear when you decided to be sitting in my room when I came out of my closet."

"If I remember right, you didn't even have the towel on." Max pointed out, and I felt my cheeks heat.

"You boys did what?" Jason growled.

"They had no idea I wasn't dressed, and I had no idea that they were there. It was an accident." I clarified. "Anyway, we went down to dinner and were surprised to find that it was a Binding Ceremony."

"You were so clever. I still don't know how you knew I was Kion's mate or that I had the potion." Mary said as she leaned more against Kion. "And I can't believe you were even willing to drink an unknown substance you were told would make the mark temporary and let Kion mark you."

"Kion seemed desperate to keep you safe. If I died, at least I helped you." I shrugged. "And if he had lied to me and he actually marked me, Cora planned on killing him." Kion looked surprised and let out a nervous chuckle. "Don't worry, you wouldn't have felt a thing." I said with a straight face and cuddled into Easton's chest. I heard the rumble of his laugh, and I smiled.

"She was in so much pain after he marked her. She nearly passed out and we escaped that night. Then we ran into you all." Mary ended the story.

I yawned and cuddled closer to Easton. "I think I am going to take Carly back to the tent to rest." Easton said to the others as he stood. I wobbled slightly and he grabbed my elbow to keep me steady. He guided me back to the tent, and once inside I noticed that there were several cots in rows.

"Which one?" I asked as I yawned.

"Our cot is over here." Easton pulled me gently and I followed him to the cot in the far corner. I laid down and curled into a ball. "Sit up for a minute, Carly." I looked at him and he smiled as he removed his shirt and handed it to me. "I think you would be more comfortable if you weren't in that dress anymore. Even though you look gorgeous in it."

I looked down and noticed I was still in the white dress I had worn at the packhouse. The bottom hem was covered in mud with several rips. The skirt and bodice had dirt smudges and small tears in the fabric. I looked back up with a raised brow. "What if I don't have any shorts on under this?"

Easton smirked. "You have shorts on. You aren't a fan of dresses and always have shorts on under them." I laughed as I stood. I turned my back to Easton and moved my hair to the side. This time he didn't hesitate to unzip my dress. When he was done, he pressed a kiss to my shoulder. I let the dress fall to the ground and pulled the shirt on quickly. "I thought you would have had an undershirt on as well." He muttered close to my ear.

    I smiled as I turned around. "I didn't need to dress in layers that morning." I laid down again and Easton climbed in beside me, laying on his back. I cuddled up to his side, rested my head on his chest, and sighed. This was my comfort. Being with Easton was heaven.

Chapter 16

The shouts of men jerked me from sleep. I sat up quickly, looking around to try to figure out what was going on. Easton was nowhere to be seen. More yelling and people running just outside the tent had me sprinting outside. A crowd was gathering on the far side of the clearing.

Panic started to build inside me. I caught Easton's scent among the gathering and headed in that direction. I shoved past people, trying to get to Easton. I needed him. I finally found him at the front, and I touched his back. He glanced down at me, and worry filled his eyes. He wrapped his arm around me, pulling me close to his side.

"Why is that man all over my son's mate?" Kain roared.

My head jerked in his direction. Fear slammed into me. There stood the man that had killed my family when I was young and had killed my mom in front of me. Easton turned so that Kain couldn't see me anymore as Mike and Max moved protectively in front of me. I hadn't even noticed them next to us.

"I demand my son's mate be returned to him." Kain yelled.

I started shaking. Easton pressed a kiss to my temple. "I won't let him anywhere near you, Carly." he whispered in my ear as I clung to him.

"That's enough, father." Kion growled. "Carly is not my mate, she never was."

"What do you mean? Your mark is on her neck. I saw you give her the mark!" Kain yelled, and I flinched.

"Mary is my mate. Alpha Callum bound us yesterday." Kion said with pride in his voice. "Carly is right where she should be. Now, why don't you turn around and leave."

"You ungrateful little..." Kain seethed. "Do you realize what you have done? You traded the most powerful she-wolf for an Omega."

"The real question is why you feel the need to break the laws of our kingdom?" Jet asked from a few feet away.

Kain's demeanor completely changed when he saw Jet. He took a step toward Jet, but Jet raised his hand to stop him.

"I don't understand what you mean." Kain said in a confused tone. "That man has stolen my son's mate. Kion and the girl had a Binding Ceremony, and he marked her a few days ago."

"Carly, come here please." Jet said as he turned to look at me. He extended his hand in invitation for me to take it. Easton's arm tightened around me, and a low growl rumbled from his chest. "It's okay, Easton. No harm will come to your mate." I grudgingly left the safety of Easton's arms and slowly walked to Jet. He put an arm over my shoulders. "Remarkable how this random girl is almost an exact copy of my sister. I think the only difference is the eye color."

Kain's eyes hardened when he looked at me. Pure hatred burned in his eyes. "Can someone explain to me what is going on?" Kain growled.

"That is exactly what I would like to know." A deep voice boomed from the side of the clearing.

Everyone turned to see an older man slowly walking from the trees with several others. The man had short dark brown hair with grey streaking through it. His whole presence radiated power. As he passed by, those closest bowed their heads. Jet let go of me and walked to meet the newcomers.

I watched as Jet embraced the older man and then another man that looked like a slightly older version of Jet. Jet spoke with them in hushed tones for a few moments before the three of them turned to look at me.

I moved uncomfortably as I stood alone in front of everyone. A hand touched my back and I glanced to see that Easton had moved to my side. Jet and the newcomers headed in our direction, stopping a few feet away. The older looking Jet reached out to touch me. Easton shoved me behind him as he growled.

Amusement flashed in the man's eyes. "You stand against me?" The man asked. "Do you know who I am?"

"I will stand between anyone and Carly, regardless if they are the future Alpha King or not." Easton stated firmly.

"You can't be more than eighteen and you are willing to lose your life for her?" The man asked.

"She is my mate; I will protect her with my life if necessary." Easton stated firmly.

My eyes widened in surprise. Easton was going against the Alpha King for me? I grabbed his arm in an attempt to get his attention, but he only grabbed my hand, giving it a quick squeeze before letting go. His attention never left the man in front of us.

There was a tense silence and then the older man standing a few feet away laughed. "It's alright boy. We mean her no harm."

Jet smiled at me. "This is my father, the Alpha King and my older brother, Toren." I slid my hand into Easton's as I moved to his side. I gripped his arm with my other hand.

"Now that we are here…Jet, will you please explain why you sent such an urgent message requesting that Toren and I both come immediately?" The Alpha King said as he continued to study me.

"Alpha Kain is claiming that his son Kion and Carly were bound together and then marked." Jet said simply.

The Alpha King turned to look at a pale Kain. "That is impossible. Any binding and marking with Carly have to be approved by one of the royal family. To my knowledge, that has not taken place."

"I never approved of such a union." Toren agreed.

"I'm sorry for interrupting, my king." Jason stepped forward and bowed. "Why does Carly's mate need to be approved by the royal family?" The Alpha King narrowed his eyes as he looked at Jason.

"This is Jason Shepherd, Gamma of the Silver Moon Pack. He is a father figure to Carly." Jet supplied. The Alpha King continued to glare at Jason.

I growled and the Alpha King looked at me. "Answer his question, Alpha King." I narrowed my eyes at him, daring him not to respond. Out of the corner of my eye I saw several people bow their heads as I continued to glare at him.

He studied me for a long moment before speaking. "Retract your aura, little one." He smiled at me, and I blinked in surprise. My aura?

"I think she is stronger than most Alphas." Jet chuckled. "I have seen you submit to your Alpha before though."

"My mom taught me to recognize the different levels of auras I was feeling, and to respond accordingly, but they don't affect me." I shrugged. "Now answer Papa Bear's question."

"That explains why you didn't react after the trial when I tried to get you to stop." Jet smiled.

The Alpha King quirked a brow before turning to Jason. "The North Wind Pack has a law that states, if there is no male heir to take over as Alpha, then the oldest daughter's mate becomes Alpha. Carly is also of royal birth and any future husband must be approved by the royal family." The Alpha King explained. "Carly is the daughter of Alpha Kyle and my daughter, by all rights, she is the Luna of the North Wind Pack."

I felt Easton tense. He looked down at me with wide eyes. His head snapped up to look at Jet when Jet started to speak. "I approved of Easton. If I had not, I would have stopped the ceremony." Jet's eyes held laughter. "When he went against his base desire to see Marissa pay for hurting you, just because you asked him to, I knew he would be good for you. A true leader will yield to someone wiser than themselves yet be willing to sacrifice everything to protect those important to them. That and even though Easton was born to the Gamma family, he has an Alpha's aura."

"This is ridiculous." Kain yelled. "That boy stole her from my son." Kain fumed.

"Carly!" Cora yelled.

I saw the flash of steel just as Kain lunged for Easton. I shoved Easton out of the way. He stumbled back a few steps before falling backwards. Kain's momentum had him slamming into me. We fell to the ground and the knife sliced along my side as we rolled. I ignored the pain and climbed onto Kain's back. He started to try to throw me. I wrapped my legs around his torso and my arm around his neck. I grabbed the crook of my other arm while placing a hand on the back of his head. I squeezed my elbows together while pushing his head down.

Kain scratched at my arms and attempted to hit my face. I ducked my head so that it was buried in his shoulder. Seconds later, Kain stopped struggling and I released my hold on him. I scooted back, breathing hard. The whole thing had only lasted a few moments. I struggled to my feet as Easton, Max, and Mike came up to me. Easton touched my side and I winced.

"What the heck were you thinking?" he asked angrily. Worry was in his eyes, and I knew he wasn't truly mad at me, just concerned for my safety.

"Get him chained up." The Alpha King ordered before stepping close to us.

"I am so tired of that man taking everyone I love from me. I'm not going to stand by and watch it happen again." I said as I looked down. Kain's knife lay on the ground. It was the same one he had used to kill mom.

Wetness on my side registered in my mind and I pulled my eyes from the knife to see why I was wet. There was a cut in Easton's shirt. "Dang it." I muttered under my breath as I lifted the hem of the shirt to see that my side was covered in blood. "Sorry for ruining your shirt." I said, lowering the shirt back down.

"You honestly think I care about the shirt when he stabbed you." Easton asked in disbelief. He pressed his hand to my wound firmly.

"Are you okay? Where did you learn to fight like that?" The Alpha King asked.

"Do not let her get you to the ground. I learned that the hard way." Jet said as he walked up. "Are you okay?"

"It's a scratch. I'm fine." I said as I moved back toward the tents, keeping my gaze on the ground. Easton continued to push on my side as we walked. The crowd parted for me and Easton, letting us pass without an issue.

As soon as I was in the tent, I pushed Easton's hand away and pulled the shirt off to get a better look at the cut. "Do you think it will need stitches?" I asked without looking up. It was hard to twist my body to get a good look at the damage.

"Carly, you can't do that." Easton's voice sounded pained. I looked up. He was standing at the tent entrance. "You could have been killed."

"I watched as he plunged a knife into mom's chest, and I wasn't going to stand there and watch as he did the same to you." I pressed the wadded-up shirt to the cut and winced.

Easton walked slowly to me. He cupped my face. "I love you, Carly. Seeing you go down with that knife aimed at you…I don't want to ever see something like that again. I am supposed to protect you." His lips pressed to mine in a desperate kiss. He pulled back and rested his forehead against mine.

"We are supposed to protect each other." I corrected him. Voices outside the tent made me aware that I was standing in just my bra and shorts. "You don't happen to have another shirt I can have, do you? Because I am feeling quite exposed at the moment." I said quietly. Easton leaned back and looked at me. His eyes darkened as a smile tugged at his lips. "Easton." I said putting my free arm across my chest as my cheeks flamed.

Easton chuckled before giving me a quick kiss. He stepped around me and pulled a bag out from under our cot. He started rummaging through it when his head snapped up, his gaze fixed on the tent door. He moved back to me quickly, wrapping his arms around me and spinning us so that his back was facing the door. A second later I heard someone walk in and I pressed myself more into Easton, trying to hide the best I could.

"I can't believe he tried to kill you." Mary said angrily. "In front of the Alpha King no less." She huffed. She went quiet for a second before clearing her throat. I realized that Easton was shirtless too. "Kion asked if I had any extra clothes you might borrow. Before we left, I shoved your clothes into my bag. I'm just going to leave them here." Mary said quickly before she practically ran from the tent.

I peeked around Easton and let out a tense breath when I saw we were alone again. I stepped around him and walked to the cot where Mary had left my clothes. There were also bandages and a first aid kit. I grabbed the kit and opened it.

Glancing over at Easton, I asked, "Do you know how to sew?"

He narrowed his eyes at me. "No."

"Time for a lesson." I sat on a nearby cot and pulled out the items we would need.

Easton had flat out refused to stitch up my side, but when he saw me doing it myself, he grudgingly changed his mind. By the time he was done, I was sweating and nauseous. It had taken twelve stitches to close the cut.

Easton wiped the blood off my skin, patted the area dry and put a clean bandage over it. He pulled me onto his lap and held me until I felt ready to get dressed. I pulled on my skinny jeans over my spandex shorts. The feel of Easton's eyes on me had me glancing in his direction. His eyes were fixed on me. I gave him a questioning look.

"I don't think I have ever seen you in anything that wasn't baggy. Well, other than your workout clothes."

I smiled at him as I slowly put my shirt on, careful not to hit my side. "That's because I wore baggy clothes so I could wear layers." I gestured to my outfit. "Now that I'm not freezing all the time, I can wear things more my style."

Easton's gaze swept over me appreciatively. "I like this new look." He said as his dimple appeared.

"I hope you two are decent." Mike called from the tent door. He stepped inside and smiled at us. "Mary said you two were uh…" His voice trailed off as his cheeks turned pink.

"I took my shirt off to see the wound better. Easton was, well, like that and he was shielding me from whoever was coming in." I clarified as I felt my own blush rising up my neck.

"How bad is it?" Mike asked, dropping his gaze to my side.

I waved off his concern. "Twelve stitches. No big deal." Easton muttered under his breath about me being impossible and downplaying my injuries.

"Good to hear that you aren't seriously hurt." Mike smiled. "The Alpha King and princes are wanting an audience with you, if you are feeling up to it."

"I guess we will have to face them sooner or later." I muttered.

"What do you think they want to talk to us about?" Cora asked.

I looked over at Easton. He had moved back to his bag and pulled a shirt from it. He put it on as he walked over to me. *"I don't know, Cora. I just hope it isn't more bad news."* I told her as Easton reached my side.

Easton's arm went around my waist and he kissed my temple. "Ready when you are, Love." He said with his lips still brushing my skin. I would never get tired of the warmth I felt every time Easton touched me.

"Mike, can you let them know that Easton and I will be there in a few minutes?" I asked, needing a few minutes without some sort of crisis. He nodded and left.

I leaned against Easton's strong chest and closed my eyes. He drew me close, resting his chin on top of my head. He seemed to sense my need to just 'be' for a few minutes. I took several deep breaths to re-center myself and let them out slowly. When I finally felt ready to face the world again, I moved back enough to see Easton. He looked down at me. I studied him.

His scruff gave him a rugged untamed look that suited him. He wore a soft smile, and his dimple was barely visible. The dark circles under his eyes showed how little sleep he had been getting lately. His dark brown hair was getting a little long. I couldn't resist the urge to run my hands through it. Easton closed his eyes at my touch, and I smiled. I rose on my toes and gave him a soft kiss.

"I love you, Easton Shepherd." His eyes popped open, and he looked at me in surprise. Slowly a smile spread on his lips before he gave me another kiss as he cupped the back of my head.

"I figured we would learn to love each other, especially since we are mates and married, but…" Easton shook his head as he continued to grin. "I mean, I have been in love with you for the past several years, but when did you...?" He watched me, eyes twinkling.

"I think I realized it when Papa Bear said you were leaving for a few days. I felt panicked and didn't want you to go." I admitted, biting my lip.

Easton chuckled. "That is why you were upset; you didn't want me to go?"

I shrugged. "I don't know. I was so confused at the time. I kept telling myself that you guys couldn't be trusted, but I felt safe and protected with you. You kissed me, which only added to my confusion as to why you guys were being all protective. Then you were leaving, and I nearly had a panic attack. You took me upstairs and just a simple hug from you calmed me. Cora and I didn't understand what was happening to me."

Easton kissed me again. I tilted my head slightly, deepening the kiss. Easton was the one that pulled back first. "I love you, Carly Shepherd."

I blinked in surprise, then laughed. I hadn't really thought about what had happened over the past several days and what it truly meant. I was now Easton Shepherd's wife, and I couldn't be happier.

Chapter 17

Easton and I stood before the Alpha King, Jet, and Toren in a circular tent that had been set up for the King. Easton was tense and held my hand tightly as we listened to the three of them discussing the North Wind Pack and what training we would need to take over.

"I love that they assume they know what we want." Cora grumbled.

"I don't want to be Luna." I told her. "And I don't want to be in an unfamiliar pack." I sighed. "I wish I had talked to Easton about this before we got here."

Easton leaned close to my ear. "Talk to me about what?" he asked in a quiet whisper.

I turned and looked at him in surprise. "What?" I whispered.

"Are we boring you two?" The Alpha King asked in irritation.

I looked at him before returning my attention back to Easton. *"Did you just hear my thoughts?"* I asked in my head. Easton's head cocked to the side as his brow drew down in confusion. *"You can hear me, can't you?"* I pressed.

"How are we mind-linking in human form?" Easton asked. *"I mean, as a member of a pack, in wolf form, we can mind-link other wolves of the pack, but I have never heard of mind-linking as humans."*

I shrugged. *"We can puzzle that out later."* I glanced over at the three royals who were watching us closely. *"Do you want to be Alpha?"* I asked Easton, returning my gaze to his face.

"Carly, this decision is yours."

"No, it is ours. I want to know if you want to be an Alpha."

Easton ran his hand down his face before he rubbed the back of his neck. *"Sweetheart, the North Wind Pack is your home pack. If you want to return to that pack, I will follow you. I have never had aspirations to be an Alpha, but I would do my best to fulfill those obligations and support you if you wish to take your rightful place as Luna."* I studied him for several minutes.

I thought about what I wanted for my future, and for my future family. I gave Easton a quick kiss before turning to face the royals.

"Were you two just...mind-linking?" Toren asked slowly.

I took a small step forward while keeping Easton's hand clasped in mine. "So, now you want us to talk?" I asked with a raised brow. Jet coughed as he put his hand over his mouth in an attempt to cover his laugh.

"Child, we are just trying to make plans for your training to take your roles as Alpha and Luna." The Alpha King stood.

"Oh, of course." I smacked the palm of my hand on my forehead. "Silly me. I forgot that we don't get a say in this conversation or our futures."

Jet couldn't hold back his laughter anymore. I glared at him until he managed to get control over himself. "I told you, father, she is just like Brooke." His eyes twinkled as he chuckled. "You are going to have your hands full with her, young Mr. Shepherd."

The Alpha King watched me for a moment. "Alright, granddaughter, what is it that you want to say?" He gestured for me to continue.

"I don't want to be Luna. I don't want to be in a pack that I am unfamiliar with. I want to be near my family." I stated firmly.

"By law, you are the rightful Luna of the North Wind Pack." Toren pointed out.

"And if my parents hadn't been killed, my little brother would be the one preparing for the Alpha role." I argued. "I don't want to be a Luna, I never have. To be honest, having a mate as a Gamma is a bit much."

Easton squeezed my hand. *"Are you sure about this, Carly?"* He mind-linked me. *"Being Luna of the second most powerful pack is huge."*

"I will not be Luna." I stated, slowly looking back at Easton. "All I want to do is go home."

"If you refuse to be Alpha and Luna, then the North Wind Pack will be left leaderless." The Alpha King sat still with no emotion showing on his face.

I raised a single brow as I put my hand on my hip. "You honestly think I would believe the Alpha King doesn't have back up plans to put leaders in place?" The corner of the King's mouth turned up in a smile.

"You are very smart, Carly." The King said kindly. "We have two options available then, since you refuse to take up the mantle of your father." He paused and I glared. He was trying to manipulate me, but it wasn't going to work. "Jet could become Alpha of the pack, or it could be passed down to the next male heir which would be, Kion."

"Kion would be an excellent Alpha, even though his father was a complete tool." I said. "I'm not sure about Jet's capabilities, but I defer to the Alpha King since you are supposed to know what is best."

I turned to walk away, but Toren's voice stopped me. "There is another order of business before you leave."

"Oh?" I asked.

"Carly, as a royal, you are expected to attend several royal functions and counsels." Toren informed me.

I smiled sweetly. "You are welcome to send us invitations and we will do our best to be there." I turned once again to leave while Toren opened and closed his mouth silently, shocked by my response.

We were almost to the door when Jet called after us. "Were you mind-linking?" I looked over my shoulder at him.

"I don't know how, but I believe we were." Easton said as he turned us back to face them and I groaned. *"Come on Carly, you and Cora have to be as curious as Conall and me. Mind-linking as humans is unheard of."* Easton said through our mind-link. He spoke aloud again. "How is that even possible?"

"You two have been feeling a portion of the mate bond since you were very young." The Alpha King looked thoughtful. "My guess is that your bond has become so strong that you have developed a mind-link with each other that is separate from the pack's mind-link. There has been some mention of such a thing happening, but not for at least a century." He watched us for several moments. "Have your wolves met yet?"

"Only the other day when Carly attacked me." Easton said.

"I'm curious." The Alpha King said slowly before standing. "Would you humor me and shift?" I gave the older man a suspicious look. "Come now. There is no harm in shifting." Jet and Toren followed us outside with puzzled expressions.

Easton pulled me a little away from the others. "Conall is excited to meet Cora." He smiled down at me. "He hasn't shut up about wanting to see her in less hostile conditions."

I laughed. "What, you mean when you aren't trying to attack my cousin?"

He kissed the tip of my nose. "Exactly." He stepped back a few steps and shifted into his wolf. His eyes were dark green and watching me. I studied his wolf for several minutes, cocking my head to the side. He was a dark grey color with one ear that was lighter than the rest of him. *"What are you waiting for, Love?"*

"I'm trying to decide if you are cuter this way or as a human." I said with a smirk.

Conall playfully growled at me, and I took off running. I could hear him coming behind me. *"You ready, Cora?"* I asked with a laugh.

"Oh, I am so ready."

Just as Conall jumped at us, I dove forward and shifted. Conall flew over our head, and I changed direction, heading back towards the crowd that had started to gather. I came to a skidding stop in front of the Alpha King followed a few moments later by Conall.

"I think you are even faster than before." Easton said as his wolf rubbed his head against Cora's.

"Or you have gotten slower." I bantered back. He nipped at my ear as he growled.

"That's insane." Max's voice caused us both to look over in his direction. "Is it common for mates to be so similar in their markings?"

"No, it's quite rare." Toren shook his head.

"You can shift back now." The Alpha King quietly said. When we finished shifting back, Easton wrapped his arms around me and kissed my cheek. "Not only is Carly's wolf light grey with a darker grey ear but Easton's is the complete opposite with dark grey coloring and a lighter ear. The ear color matches the other's fur coat."

I looked up at Easton as he looked down at me. He winked and I smiled. "Man, it would have been so awkward looking so similar if I had rejected you." I stepped out of his arms quickly and his eyes narrowed.

"If you had rejected him, then I could have applied for the position." Max pouted. "Why didn't you? Now I'm going to have to find excuses to visit you guys every night." Jason stepped up to Max and smacked him on the back of his head. "Ouch." Max rubbed the spot that was hit. "Oh, come on Jason. You've tasted her cooking."

"You heard what they were saying, Easton and Carly are to be the Alpha and Luna of the North Wind Pack." Jason's expression was stiff, and sadness filled his eyes as he looked at me.

I jogged over to Jason and gave him a hug. He held me tight and pressed a kiss to my head. "You know." I looked up at him with a serious expression. "I could never leave my Papa Bear."

"What?" Jason asked, confused.

Easton made it over to us, along with Holly, Mike, and Max. "Carly and I have chosen to stay in the Silver Moon Pack. We want to remain close to family." Holly cried and threw her arms around me. Jason hugged us both as Easton looked on. "You are still the favorite." He said, crossing his arms over his chest.

I stepped away from Jason and Holly to put my arms around Easton's neck. He uncrossed his arms and put them around me. I flinched when he brushed against my injured side.

"You can't blame them for liking me more." I told him with a sweet smile. "I mean, I did take down a royal while I was sick and not feeling good, all before I fully shifted." Easton's lips twitched at the corners as he fought a smile while he tried to keep a serious expression.

Before he could say anything, Max spoke up. "Carly can cook, is a fierce fighter, crazy smart to have graduated early, took over her interview with the pack council, and is of royal descent. What have you done, East?"

Mike laughed. "When you put it that way, I think I like Carly better too."

Easton scowled at his friends, but his smile broke through. "I do have an amazing wife." Easton smiled down at me before kissing me. Max made a gagging sound, which ended in him getting smacked by Jason again.

I turned in Easton's arms and leaned back against him. I smiled as I watched the bantering between Mike and Max. My gaze shifted over to Jason and Holly as they wore smiles and shook their heads at everyone. These people were the most important people in my life. They were my family.

Easton nuzzled me before kissing his mark on my neck, causing a shiver to run down my spine. I had definitely made the right decision to return to Silver Moon. Family was everything to me.

Epilogue

Five years later.

"Where is he?" River pouted in frustration.

I watched as my daughter fisted her little hands as she paced the living room. She was such a daddy's girl. Her green eyes, so much like her father's, flashed with irritation. Her light brown hair was pulled back into two braids that made her look so sweet and innocent, a total opposite to how willful and devious she was.

I smiled. Even at the young age of four, River had a fiery personality that Easton frequently accused me of passing down to her. "River, honey. Your dad is on his way. He and Uncle Max had a meeting, remember?" I told her gently, even though I too was anxious for Easton to get home soon.

I had been having contractions all day and they were growing stronger and more uncomfortable. Another contraction hit and I took several slow, deep breaths. River furrowed her brows as she studied me.

"Mommy, are you okay?" she asked in concern.

The contraction ended and I nodded. "Just feeling a little tired." River climbed on my lap and snuggled up to me. "Would you like to have a sleepover at grandpa and grandma's house tonight?" I asked her.

River sat up straighter. Her grin was nearly ear to ear. "Oh fun! Papa makes popcorn while we watch movies." River jumped off my lap. "I go pack." River ran up the stairs and slammed her bedroom door.

I laughed. Her bag was already packed, she just needed to grab it. I picked up my phone and sent a text to Holly, asking if she could come within the hour to pick up River for a sleepover. We had talked about this plan a few weeks ago so that I wouldn't have to worry about River when the time came to have the baby.

The front door opened a few minutes later. Easton and Max walked into the front room deep in conversation.

"Daddy!" River yelled as she ran down the stairs.

"There's my princess." Easton caught River as she jumped off the bottom step, her backpack falling to the floor.

"Are you going somewhere?" Max asked teasingly as he tugged on one of River's braids.

"Mommy said I get to have a sleepover at grandpa's house." River said excitedly.

Easton's head snapped in my direction. *"Is this a normal sleep over or THE sleepover?"* He asked through our mind-link.

Another contraction hit and I sucked in a quick breath. "Mommy's been doing that all day." River commented, wrinkling her little nose.

Max's eyes widened. "Would you like me to take her to your parents' house?" he asked, glancing warily at me.

"Thanks, Max. I think that would be for the best." Easton said, pressing a kiss to our daughter's cheek and setting River down. "Grab your bag, honey, and go with your uncle. Remember to be good for your grandparents."

River excitedly chatted with Max as they walked out the front door. Easton was at my side by the time the front door closed behind them. "Don't look so worried, East." I smiled at him. "It's not like this is the first time we have done this."

Easton helped me stand. I pressed a hand to my swollen belly. "I think we should get you to the pack hospital." Easton said anxiously as he carefully guided me to the door.

      *   *   *

I was lying in the hospital bed, exhausted. I looked over at my husband as he held a bundle of blankets. He was staring down adoringly at the baby he cradled. He glanced up at me and smiled. He moved to my side and pressed a kiss to my forehead.

"He has your eyes." Easton commented quietly.

I laughed. "After causing me so much trouble, he better have something of mine. Especially since River got your eyes and hair." Easton settled onto the hospital bed beside me before setting our son into my arms.

His arms went around me, and I leaned into him. "He may have my eyes, but I think he looks more like you."

The rest of the night was relatively calm but not restful. Nurses came in and looked over the baby and me constantly. Easton never left my side. When morning came, I felt ready to go home. I was tired of the constant interruptions of the nurses and the beeping of the machines.

A knock came on our door before it opened slowly. Max and Mike stepped into the room with smiles. "So, is it another girl?" Max asked. "Because I don't think this pack can handle another one of Carly's mini-mes."

I laughed, but before Easton or I could say anything, the door opened again. Jason and Holly came in, holding onto River's hands.

When she saw us, she pulled free of her grandparents and raced over to Easton. "Grammy said that I have a new brother or sister." she said in a loud whisper. "Can I see it?"

Easton chuckled as he lifted River and sat down next to me on the bed, River in his lap. She leaned over to see her little brother in my arms.

"Meet your brother, Kyson." I smiled at her. "Would you like to hold him?" River nodded slowly with wide eyes. I placed Kyson gently into her arms, Easton helping her support the baby's head.

"Oh, thank goodness it's a boy." Max put a hand to his heart dramatically. Jason smacked the back of his head and we all laughed. "What? Between Carly and River, I think we have enough troublemakers as it is."

"Your son is just as much of a troublemaker as River is, if not more." I pointed out.

Max shrugged. "I blame that on River's influence."

Easton scoffed. "Paxton is always teasing River until she loses her temper and strikes back."

"Who does that sound like, well except the striking back part?" Mike laughed. "Pax and Riv remind me so much of you and Carr."

River stared at her brother with a thoughtful expression on her face. "Mommy, do we get to keep him?"

I smiled. "Yes, River. We are keeping Kyson. He is a part of our family."

"Don't worry, Kyson. I will protect you." River whispered as she hugged him.

Easton kissed my head as I leaned into him. Sighing, I looked around the room. Our family was growing. Max and his mate, Jackie, had two little boys while Mike and his mate, Margret, had a daughter. Kion and Mary had three little girls and the North Wind Pack was flourishing under his guardianship. We regularly got together to strengthen the connection between our two packs and our families.

Max and Mike moved closer to the bed to get a better look at Kyson. I never would have thought that one of the three boys that had tormented me throughout my childhood would end up being my mate while the others were my surrogate brothers.

"You mentioned a few weeks ago that the names you picked were special to you." Holly commented. "What is the significance of the name Kyson?"

Easton smiled down at our kids before looking up at me, then settling his gaze on his parents. "Kyson is named after both his grandfathers, Kyle and Jason." I watched as Jason's eyes welled with tears.

Easton put his arm around me while he continued to help River hold Kyson. *"I love you, Carly."* he mind-linked. His voice had a hint of teasing to it. *"Even if they all end up with your fiery, impossible personality."* I scowled up at him and he pressed his lips to mine in a tender kiss.

We were discharged not long after. Everyone gathered at our house to welcome Kyson to the family and pack. I watched from the couch as Jason proudly showed off his grandson.

Easton smiled as he came and sat down next to me. I laid my head on his shoulder and looked up into his green eyes. "Have I told you lately how much I love you?" I asked in a quiet voice.

Easton chuckled. "I love you too, Sweetheart." He buried his face in my neck and pressed a kiss to his mark, causing me to shiver. I could feel his smile against my skin. "Baby, are you cold?" Easton whispered. I fought the urge to shiver as Easton kissed the mark again. I lost and a shiver ran down my spine causing Easton to laugh. "It's a good thing you have such a great heater."

I laughed and snuggled closer to him. I spotted Max across the room making a gagging motion as Paxton and River giggled. Callum smacked Max on the back of the head which only made the kids laugh harder. Easton and I joined in on the laughter. I looked up into Easton's face. He and our kids were my everything. And I wouldn't trade them for the world.

THE END

The Hunter Guardian Series

The Hunted Guardian
The Stone's Keeper
The Stone's Secret

Other books by this author:

Left Broken
Embracing Dove
Hoodwinked

When Worlds Collide

When Worlds Collide
Prey of the Corrupted Alpha

Paranormal Romance

Enforcer's Mark

www.ingramcontent.com/pod-product-compliance
Lightning Source LLC
LaVergne TN
LVHW012022060526
838201LV00061B/4416